Joe Pemberton was born in Moss Side, Manchester in 1960. His parents emigrated from the West Indies to England in the late fifties, before moving to Ashton-under-Lyne in 1970. He has worked as an electrical engineer and a college lecturer. *Forever and Ever Amen* is his first novel.

Praise for *Forever and Ever Amen*:

'An unusually intelligent and beautiful childhood memoir set in Manchester's Moss Side at the end of the sixties ... *Forever and Ever Amen* describes the adventures of nine-year-old James, in the months before his family move "up in the world" to Ashton-under-Lyne. The young hero's vivid imagination blends reality with dreams, nightmare and fantasy, creating a world of bright colour, sensory delight and innocent glee ... The real delight is Pemberton's easy musical prose. Mundane episodes are twisted through James' eyes into fantastic Hollywood adventures and the dialogue sparkles with natural wit ... Much of the charm of the novel is in its innocence and lack of cynicism' *The Big Issue in the North*

'There are many good reasons to read this book, not least for its insights into a community still little understood in Britain, and for a portrait of Moss Side far removed from its usual "guns 'n' gangs" image. Pemberton's real gift, though, is his evocation of childhood, comical yet never patronising, instantly recognisable to anybody, of whatever culture. Sense of place is strong, and yet the end result is a kind of Mancunian magic realism, strange but familiar, able to hint at large themes even in a small-scale or domestic setting. And best of all, it's also very, very funny' *Third Alternative*

'Pemberton's novel magically recreates a childhood filled with music and fun, sorrow and scrapes' *Belfast Telegraph*

'A lovely book . . . a captivating read' *Woman 2 Woman*

'A magical depiction of childhood' *Manchester Evening News*

'A first novel with real warmth and an unusual take on childhood' *What's on in Birmingham*

Forever and Ever Amen

Joe Pemberton

REVIEW

Copyright © 2000 Joe Pemberton

The right of Joe Pemberton to be identified as the Author of
the Work has been asserted by him in accordance with
the Copyright, Designs and Patents Act 1988.

First published in Great Britain in 2000
by REVIEW

An imprint of Headline Book Publishing

First published in paperback in 2000

10 9 8 7 6 5 4 3 2 1

All rights reserved. No part of this publication may be
reproduced, stored in a retrieval system, or transmitted,
in any form or by any means without the prior written
permission of the publisher, nor be otherwise circulated
in any form of binding or cover other than that in which
it is published and without a similar condition being
imposed on the subsequent purchaser.

All characters in this publication are fictitious and any
resemblance to real persons, living or dead, is purely coincidental.

ISBN 0 7472 6241 1

Typeset by Avon Dataset Ltd, Bidford-on-Avon, Warks

Designed by Ben Cracknell Studios, Norwich

Printed and bound in Great Britain by
Clays Ltd, St Ives plc

Headline Book Publishing
A division of Hodder Headline
338 Euston Road
London NW1 3BH

www.reviewbooks.co.uk
www.hodderheadline.com

For Mum, Dad and Florence – of course!

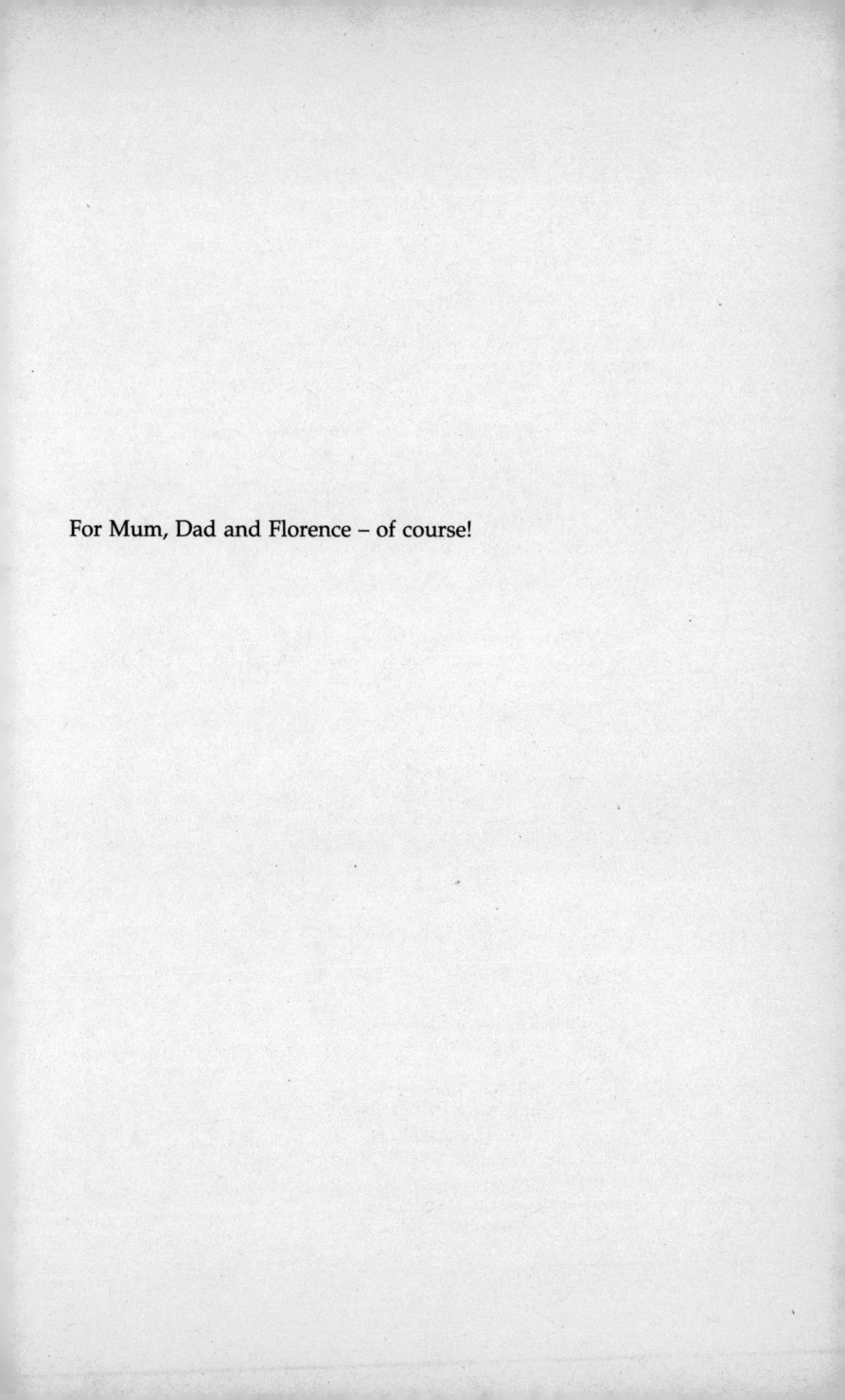

Special thanks are due to the following:

To the tutors Richard Francis, Michael Schmidt and fellow students on the 1996/97 MA in Novel Writing at Manchester University, with extra special thanks to Lynne Taylor and Susanna Jones.

To Bill Hamilton and Geraldine Cooke for having the balls to take the book on in the first place, and to Mary-Anne Harrington for showing patience, understanding and support in guiding this absolute beginner and his pile of papers into something resembling a publishable book.

And finally to the staff at the On the Eighth Day café for serving up the best value pot of tea in the whole of Manchester.

Preface

If James had his way it wouldn't be a novel. If he had his way it would be a record, a single, a Phil Spector 'Wall of Sound' with a Motown bass and drum. It would be Number One for nine weeks running, then it would have to be on the Christmas Day edition of *Top of the Pops*. Yes, if James had his way it would not be a novel.

If Aunty Mary had her way it would be the Saturday matinée down at the Wycliffe Cinema: tuppence ha'penny for the ordinary seats, a bob for the Pullman specials at the back where you could cuddle up with Arthur, imagining he was Rhett Butler in *Gone with the Wind*. Or cry your eyes out to *Now Voyager* when Bette Davis tells Paul Henreid: Don't ask for the moon: we have the stars, sniff! Yes, if Aunty Mary had her way.

Trouble is, she hasn't, neither has James, as I'm always telling them. It's me that's holding the pen, it's me that stares at a blank computer screen hour after hour instead of having a life. It's me, myself, I, Joseph Emmanuel Pemberton, Ashton-under-Lyne, Lancashire, England, United Kingdom, Europe, Earth, the Universe, the Galaxy, the Milky Way . . .

'The Mars Bar, the Bounty, the Toffee Crisp ...' says James, sticking his nose in yet again. James has always been there, I can't ever remember a time when he wasn't. He was the perfect companion when you were the only boy in a houseful of sisters, mums, aunts and female cousins, but absolutely of no use whatsoever when you're on the wrong side of thirty-nine years old, and counting. He's lousy company too when you're about to sign the deeds for a three-storey terraced house when what you really want to do is to curl up in the corner, any corner, and suck your thumb until the bad man goes away.

'River Deep,' says Aunty Mary.

'River Deep?' says James.

'And Mountain High, we mustn't forget the Mountain High. Where would we be without the Mountain High?' says Aunty Mary.

'Yeah, yeah, yeah,' says James.

Whenever I hear that record the memories come flooding back. Old terraced houses on cobbled streets, Belle Vue Fair, billy bread with bits of pork in the middle, caterpillars in a jar, Sunday school, mice in the kitchen, cockroaches in the bathroom, ice-cream cornets with chocolate strawberry syrup chopped nuts hundreds and thousands and still have change from a bob for *Whizzer and Chips*. Whether I'm driving on the motorway or preparing lesson plans for tomorrow's class I have to stop a while to let the mist fall from my eyes.

I tell James there are many advantages to the story being a novel; you can use over fifty thousand words for example.

'Fifty thousand words, wow, that's big!' says James, picking his nose.

'How many times have I told you, James,' says Aunty Mary. 'Disgusting habit.'

'Sorry, Aunty Mary,' says James.

I try again. I tell him you can employ all kinds of nuances and subplots, multi-layered subtexts sublimated to an unconscious level, all of which are necessary when trying to convey the reasons for a black family moving from Moss Side to Ashton-under-Lyne in the late 1960s.

'And you believe that, do you?' says Aunty Mary. 'Talk about a load of crap!'

'Oh Aunty Mary, you swore!!' says James.

'Crap isn't swearing,' says Aunty Mary.

'Oh yes it is,' says James.

'No it isn't. Besides, it's not as bad as picking your nose.'

'Oh yes it is.'

'Oh no it isn't.'

'Oh yes it is.'

I suggest writing the story as a pantomime. I wait for the laughter. There's none coming.

'Poor boy,' says Aunty Mary, 'I don't think he can help it.'

I tell them there's no story anyway, not the way they tell it. It's all bits and pieces, just little stories one by one. Okay by themselves, but not as a novel. A novel must have structure, a narrative form, a plot; a novel must have a plot. Aunty Mary puts her knitting down.

'If it's a plot you want, go find an allotment.'

'You're dead funny you, Aunty Mary,' says James.

'Why thank you, young man,' says Aunty Mary, reaching for the basket by the side of her chair. 'Chocolate eclair?'

'Yes please, Aunty Mary.'

Needless to say, she doesn't offer me any.

I tell them it doesn't matter how many weird and wonderful adventures they have, it's still all over the place, like a bad haircut. It will never be published neither, not the way they tell it. No publisher in their right mind will look at such a book. And what's the use of writing a book if it's not published, I say. And if someone's stupid enough to publish the damn thing then there's the agents and their ten per cent, book cover designs, book launches, readings, and other such nonsense. Knowing my luck, I say, it'll become a best-seller.

'Publishers? Agents? Best-sellers, eh?' says Aunty Mary. 'My my, young man, you'll be wanting jam on it next.'

'Jam?' says James. 'You've got jam? Wow wee.'

Aunty Mary reaches into her basket and takes out a pot of home-made strawberry jam, hot buttered scones and a bottle of fizzy lemonade.

'Pass me your glass, James.'

'Wow,' says James, 'it's just like a picnic.'

Mary looks at me and smiles. 'I wouldn't worry too much, young man, it'll be okay, you'll see.' Then she offers me a glass. 'Lemonade?'

one

'Once upon a time, indeed. Try again and this time a bit more Oomph!'

... The plane crashed into Greenheys School bursting everything into flames. Houses collapsed, babies screamed, mothers wailed and old men prayed, until all that was left was the old prefab at the corner of Great Western Street. To round things off, Mr Meskie's ice-cream van sped round the corner playing 'Stardust' by Nat King Cole. It stopped right in front of James's house.

'Mum!?!'

'Me purse is over the fireplace,' said Mum, sewing bras and girdles for Mr Mackenzie. It took a whole week to earn five pounds. Every week-day up at seven-thirty, before the kids got up to make their own breakfast. A stop for a cup of tea at ten-thirty, a habit she picked up from when she worked piecework at Smiths in Brookes Bar. Then it was head down and no stopping until two o'clock then prepare the dinner for tonight. Mondays and Tuesdays, chop the chicken and leave the rice and peas to soak. Wednesday, put the potatoes yams carrots dumplings sweet potatoes and green bananas to boil with mutton for soup. Thursdays, fry the fish and make up the dough for janny cakes, making an extra big one for Raymond because he liked his janny cakes extra big. Fridays, half a crown for five lots of fish and chips after doing the shopping at the supermarket which was usually no problem because Fridays was when Mr Mackenzie would come round in his little grey van with more work and an envelope with five pounds, or less if she'd made any mistakes. It was a good job Raymond paid the gas and electricity and other things like that or else there wouldn't be enough money for anything, not even fish and chips.

Still, yesterday's letter from the estate agents had cheered her up. Just think, by the end of the summer, no more cockroaches in the kitchen, no donkey-stoning the doorstep and no more kerb-crawlers. 'Look straight ahead and keep walking. If they ask you how much, tell them you'll scream and call for the police,' said Aunty Mary, a next-door neighbour who had lived on Cadogen Street forever and ever amen. But James had more important things to do.

'A double ninety-nine with strawberry chocolate two wafers nuts hundreds and thousands, please!'

James was about to suck the last bit of ice-cream through the bottom of the cone, when suddenly next door opened and out came Aunty Mary wearing a hairnet, night-gown and fluffy pink slippers. Mum insisted you call all the old people either Aunty or Uncle even if they weren't. James didn't mind with Aunty Mary. She always gave him sweets and cakes. 'Come inside, young man. I've something for you.'

For a nine-year-old, James had seen a great deal. Three men on the moon in a basket and three balloons, Jennifer's mum bash the living daylights out of Dave Higgins's dad, and a man killed on Great Western Street. It wasn't a man, really, just the lollipop man. A van ran him down and broke his head all over the road. Classes were cancelled and everyone went home, it was great. James had seen a great deal but never a budgerigar's funeral. Joey was its name. They were burying it in Aunty Mary's backyard: a bricked-up pile of dirt with plants, flowers and a small bush with yellow caterpillars.

♪The Lord is my shepherd, I shall not want♪ sang Aunty Mary, still in the hairnet, night-gown and pink fluffy slippers. 'If Arthur had been alive, flush it down the loo he'd say.'

'The loo?' asked James.

Aunty Mary's face went as pink as her slippers.

'The loo, you know, the Jimmy, the lav, you know.'

She continued to sing, this time in descant. ♪*In pastures green He leadeth me* . . .♪ 'James, did I ever tell you Joey could talk?'

She said a lot of things did Aunty Mary. A brass band played in Alexandra Park every Sunday lunchtime. The supermarket on Moss Lane East was a lake with goldfish in it.

'There's a bomb across the road on Fernleaf Street just waiting to go *boom*.'

Aunty Mary said a lot of things. Still, she made lovely cakes and pies.

'Your mother tells me you'll be moving soon.'

'Yes, Aunty Mary, I'll come back and visit.'

'Don't mind yourself with an old woman like me. Besides, you'll be making new friends.'

'Mum says there's a garden.'

'That's nice.'

'And two trees, one at the front, one at the back.'

'Arthur would've loved a house with a garden but things didn't quite work out.'

'Things? What things?'

'Things, you know, just things.'

'I'll come back to see you, honest, every week even.'

'Of course you will, dear. And I'll make your favourite: apple pie custard and a nice cup of tea,' said Aunty Mary.

'Umm lovely,' said James.

'Goldfinger' by Shirley Bassey. You know the beginning: big orchestral extravaganza followed by wah-wah trumpets in four parts; the first two loud and brassy, the last two soft and soothing. Just the beginning, mind you, over and over again like the needle had stuck. After a while you forgot Miss Bassey was ever in it, never mind James Bond. The music went well with the big black cars parked outside Aunty Mary's house. James was in a quandary. Should he go over and tell them she wasn't in, or what? Aunty Mary hadn't been in for a long time now, not since the time the milk bottles stayed on her doorstep all day.

The air became heavy like a bag of ball bearings and it began to rain – you know, one of those heavy downpours that grew water-flowers as high as the window sill. James was okay, though, snug comfy cosy and wrapped in musty old curtains in the paraffin warmth of Mum's sewing room. The drum drum drumming of the sewing machine went well with the line of black cars **and wah-wah trumpets.** And as people-in-black ran indoors from the rain **the trumpets became softer, almost silent, out of respect.**

If it was up to James, he'd have the Four Tops doing a slow dance like on *Top of the Pops*. **Or even the Temptations. They'd be dressed in black suits too and be groovy like the Four Tops because you had to be groovy to be on** *Top of the Pops*. The people-in-black didn't look keen though. They weren't in the mood for anything much, except a cup of tea perhaps, and some custard creams.

The people-in-black eventually came out again, only now they were carrying a coffin with shiny handles. Then they placed it inside the longest black car which had a board covered with a green tablecloth. Then one by one the cars drove off and from the safety of the musty old curtains. James watched until the last car disappeared into **the mist at the end of the road.**

If James listened carefully, yes, **tingly tambourines, in between the orchestra, trumpets and everything else.** He could do that, dead easy; tingle the tambourines. Getting one would be dead easy. There were loads in the church that no one would miss. He'd be ready the next time, with his tingly tambourine. The next time the milk bottles stayed on Aunty Mary's doorstep all day and people-in-black pretended to cry before driving off for more tea and biscuits.

Mum continued to sew as if nothing had happened, drum drumming on the sewing machine, five pounds still being so hard to earn.

Suddenly the sun came out and in seconds everything was dried to a sunny summer's day. The trumpets went back to being loud and brassy, just like Shirley Bassey.

'A million Mo-Jos, *Whizzer and Chips* for hundreds of weeks, a double ninety-nine with twist cone strawberry chocolate syrup nuts hundreds and thousands every day for the rest of your life . . .'

James's favourite game. What he would buy if he won the pools. Now it was even more fun being accompanied by a full orchestra.

'A houseful of gobstoppers ♪waaah wah, a zillion bags of fish and chips wah waaah wah♭, that Scalectrix set in the toy shop on Denmark Road . . .'

Raymond wasn't in the mood for this. All he wanted was to drink his brown ale and watch the evening news. Was it too much to ask for? He'd been up since five, same time every week-day. Then three buses to work, and the same three back and if there were no breakdowns or full buses or traffic jams then he was home for seven-thirty, in time for dinner, if he was lucky. So it wasn't too much to ask for, some peace and quiet. But would James shut up?

'Dad, is it a hundred miles to Ashton-under-Lyne?'

Mr Hagen, the man at the estate agents, had been most insistent.

'I cannot envisage any problems, not on your wages.'

And when he asked about the solicitors, Mr Hagen wasn't much help there neither.

'I'll sort that out for you.'

And as for the deposit for the house, well, where on earth would he find all that money?

'No problem,' said Mr Hagen. 'There should be enough when you sell your house.' And when he asked but what if no one buys our house, Veronica rolled her eyes and looked to the ceiling and Mr Hagen smiled.

'I wouldn't worry if I was you.' Then Mr Hagen passed Raymond a fountain pen from his jacket pocket.

'I need both your signatures if you don't mind.'

'Dad?'

Was it too much to ask for at the end of the week, some peace and quiet? Not that he wasn't grateful. At least there was a wage at the end of every week, unlike back home where you only got paid in the crop season when sugarcane needed cutting. The good jobs such as a teacher or in the bank went to half-castes or children who wore shoes to school.

'Is it two hundred miles, Dad?'

And at the end of every month it was straight to the Post Office for ten pounds of postal orders for his mother and brothers and sisters back home. Well, it used to be, until Veronica put her foot down after they returned from their holiday of a lifetime. So was it too much to ask for, a glass of warm brown ale and some peace and quiet?

'Dad!!!'

'No James, not *that* far.'

Kids, you'd think they'd be grateful with it being Friday night. Two packets of crisps, roast chicken flavour. Friday nights was sweets night. Crunchies, Smarties, or even Toffee Crisps, one each, of course, or else there would be a fight. After eating all those sweets you would think he would be grateful. But not James, oh no!

'Mum says it takes three buses.'

'Your mother says a lot of things.'

Yes, Veronica said a lot of things. She asked for a lot as well. It wasn't as if he never tried. Hadn't he taken to Felicia like she was his own daughter when she first came? He hadn't argued when Veronica demanded they should send for her. In fact he'd insisted.

'Yes, I think so too,' he'd said at the time and he meant it too.

'Dad, will our tree have yellow caterpillars, Dad, caterpillars, our tree, Dad?'

It was only ten pounds a month. Was it too much to ask for? It was for his mother, for heaven's sake. He couldn't stop the money just like that, not without a fight. Didn't he always pay the bills on time? The electricity, the gas, the man from Royal Victoria. No policeman ever came round to their house, for heaven's sake. Of course he shouldn't have hit Veronica, it wasn't right. Even so, it wasn't as if it was the first time, it wasn't as if he was the only one neither. He didn't know anyone who hadn't hit their wife at least once in a while. Even his father did, when he was around. But this time Veronica had meant it; she wasn't coming back if he hit her again, children or no children.

A holiday of a lifetime, indeed. A holiday of a lifetime his foreman had said when he allowed Raymond to have four weeks off in one go. It took a lifetime to save up for it, but Veronica had insisted. 'You want to go back as poor as you left or what?'

Four weeks, three at his mother's house in Nevis and the first week at Veronica's grandmother. Veronica had insisted. 'You have all your brothers and sisters to see and I haven't any.'

If Raymond had known what it would be like at her grandmother's house he would've happily stayed an extra couple of days to help out. He'd have fixed up a few things here and there, the wall, the roof, put in a new window, bought some corn, and made up a new fence all around the house to stop the chickens escaping. Raymond was good at mending things, anything in wood. When he was boy, Mr Henderson, a neighbour, had taught him carpentry. Roofs, walls, fences, anything. Maurice, Mr Henderson's son, was too busy studying for school and college for his father to teach him carpentry. Which was fine by Raymond because Mr Henderson would pay him two dollars for a day's work.

It wasn't easy for Veronica's grandmother, looking after all those grandchildren at her age. Veronica was almost in tears when they left. And she didn't say anything until they arrived at the airport.

'I can't leave them like that,' she said, and she didn't say another word until the plane landed at Heathrow. Nothing had been the same ever since. If only the foreman had said no, you can't have four weeks off. Then they wouldn't have had that holiday of a lifetime and that would've been it. If only the foreman had insisted, if only.

If only James would shut up and let him have some peace and quiet.

The man wore a Brylcreem suit with a flower sticking out of the left-side buttonhole. The woman wore a white wedding dress and a pink bouquet with a horseshoe for good luck. Just like the colour tinted photograph that used to be on Aunty Mary's mantelpiece. But the man and woman weren't indoors, they were dancing in the street like Ginger Rogers and Fred Astaire. The woman looked so pretty and as light as a feather, so light a gust of wind or even a door slamming would blow her away. Not that

it could even if it wanted to because the man in the Brylcreem suit was holding on to her like he wanted to stay with her forever and ever, amen. Not even the cobbles in the streets could put them off their step. Another one of Aunty Mary's stories. The one where the cobbled streets were filled with horse-driven carts and a herd of stampeding cows on their way to the butcher's.

'Time for bed, young man. Up the stairs, apples and pears.'

'Aw Mum, they've not finished.'

'Okay, five more minutes.'

Mum thought it was best to play along at moments like this. Besides, she could do another D-cup before he was done.

James felt peckish. One of Aunty Mary's fairy cakes would be ideal right now. She called them butterfly cakes because they had bits of pastry stuck into the icing on top, just like butterfly wings. They couldn't fly, of course, not like Joey. Aunty Mary would let him out of the cage and he'd fly all over the room and bump into things. Just like the time when James opened the cage while Aunty Mary was in the bathroom. Joey flew right into the wedding photo on the mantelpiece and knocked it to the floor. It was all right, though, the picture wasn't broke. Joey was still flapping his wings as James carefully placed his body back in the cage. **It was then James heard the plane crashing outside . . .**

The night sky became a blue-green stream of yellow dotted stars with a milk-bottle top for the moon. The smell of freshly baked bread, roast chicken and exhaust fumes from the ice-cream van wafted through the air like Christmas Day. And the streetlights flickered like a great

big fireworks on Bonfire Night and their reflection off the cobbled stones was like a thousand and one cats' eyes.

'This is perfect, just perfect.'

Then the curtains closed all by themselves and Mum spoke softly. 'Up the stairs, apples and pears.'

And as if by magic James was in his pyjamas and being tucked into bed. He had one more question before the Sandman arrived. 'Will we live happily ever after in our new house, Mum?'

She didn't answer right away. She sat down on the bed, as if in another world. Then she kissed him on the forehead. 'Of course we will, love. Of course.'

two

'Pickles, pineapples, *Party Sevens??*'

Aunty Vernice was James's favourite aunty even though one of her fingers was missing. She accidentally cut it off when she was chopping wood or something. The left hand, smallest finger. An ugly little stump it was, like it forgot to grow. Every visit she brought ice-cream. Either ten scoopfuls in a big bowl or a cornet each.

'When I win the pools I'll take you to the West Indies, back to St Kitts, back *home*.' Every time she said back *home* she had that look in her eye like she'd lost a puppy. James had got all excited and told all his friends at school. But when she didn't win the pools the next week, or the next, or the next one after that, he decided that when he grew up he would never do the pools. She was still his favourite aunt though. She also served great food at her parties, even though one of her fingers was missing.

There was one tonight, Saturday night. Aunty Vernice's parties were always on Saturday nights. In the front room was a whole table full of party goodies. Not only sandwiches, crisps and nuts, but also sausages, cheese, pickles, pineapples, all on sticks. As well as the food-on-sticks there were always the plates full of fried chicken, lemonade bottles full of rum and piles of Party Sevens stacked to the roof. The food was great at Aunty's parties. Trouble was, the food table was always in the front room with the music and the grown-ups, who thought nothing of making nine-year-old boys dance in front of everyone so they could have a good laugh.

'Why is it always me?'

The other little cousins stared at James with hungry eyes. They wanted feeding and it was his duty to go for the food now he was the oldest. Felicia was old enough to go with the grown-ups. It was no use Laura going. She'd only stand there crying. Still, no one lifted her up or kissed her on the cheeks and said how cute she was, so maybe she wasn't as daft as she made out.

When he grew up, no one would be banished to the back room at parties. There would be a food table just for the kids, with cheese and pickled onions, sandwiches, fish and chips, hamburgers and saveloys, all of them on sticks. There'd also be a big bowl of Smarties, and telly just for the kids and they could leave it on as long as they liked.

The music boomed along the distant corridor mixed in with loud shouting and laughter. James felt sick. Not as sick as having liver boiled potatoes cabbage and semolina for dinner, but it wasn't far off. Still, he had no choice. Laura was about to burst into tears, then he'd really be in trouble.

The narrow corridor came to life like a long slithery snake woken from a bad dream. The wallpaper gave off a bad-tempered whiff of damp and cat pee. The music and shouting came frighteningly nearer with each step. As he got closer to the front room more grown-ups appeared. First in singles, propping up a bottle of brown ale to their lips without spilling a drop, and then in pairs, chewing each other's ears like they didn't know there was food in the front room.

As James pushed open the front door, a blast of sweat, aftershave and Johnson's baby powder almost knocked him out. But he'd made it and he was still alive. The noise was now unbearable of course. A mixture of the Mighty Sparrow, Alma Cogan and a class of kids when there was no teacher about. But there was only one thing on his mind. In the corner by the window, like an ice-cream van in the middle of the school playground, was the food. Hallelujah.

Nothing would stop James now. There could be an earthquake or even an arithmetic test every day of the week. Even if he climbed Mount Everest without his shoes or socks, nothing could describe the sense of achievement he felt. However, there was still the descent, and he'd forgotten what everyone had wanted. Was it Garibaldi biscuits or custard creams for Anthea? As he was piling his second plate high he felt a tap on his shoulder.

'Here, let me give you a hand.' It was Mum. 'How about some more janny cakes.'

James wanted to pinch himself to see if he was dreaming. This was all going so smoothly. Too smoothly perhaps. Something had to go wrong. And sure enough a familiar voice boomed from the dancing crowd.

'Coolie, come back. I have not finished yet, woman.'

James turned round half expecting a cornet with double

ninety-nine and strawberry syrup. But the last thing on Aunty Vernice's mind was ice-cream for James.

'Coolie, did you hear me, woman!'

This wasn't the curler-haired scarfed old lady that promised James a trip to the West Indies.

'Get back here!'

'Want a drink, James? Some beer?' said Mum, trying hard to ignore the shouting.

That only made Aunty Vernice shout louder. 'Don't walk away when I'm talking, stupid fool.'

'Can't you see I'm helping the boy?'

'Raymond, tell your wife to get back here now. Coolie!!!'

'Here James, have a Party Seven. Don't let your Dad see.'

'Veronica!!! Didn't you hear me, woman?'

'I'll help you carry them to the back room. We'll have our own party there, eh? Don't forget the cups.'

The couples had stopped chewing each other's ears and were now staring at Mum and Aunty Vernice like they were someone famous off the telly.

When they did eventually reach the back room with all the other kids, Mum told them stories. Not embarrassing ones about James, thank goodness, but ones about a little girl in the West Indies whose mother had died and whose father loved her but couldn't look after her because he had his own children, who lived with her aunt who loved her but couldn't show it because she had her own children and who came to England to look for love and was still looking.

She also went on about other adventures, some really exciting ones with people falling off mountains and a man who chopped up little boys with an axe. Normally James would be too embarrassed having to listen to his mum's stories in front of everyone else. Tonight he didn't mind. In fact, he really couldn't give a damn. Two glasses of Party Seven had that effect.

three

'There but for the *Grace* of God. It's a joke, James, a pun – oh forget it.'

Grace was too big to speak to James. She was even too big to speak to Felicia and her big girlfriends. She was so big she could talk to Mum on the corner of Cadogen Street and Broadfield Road without asking permission first. Even so, she would always find the time to look down and say *hello James*. Not today though. All she could do was sigh. Mum was no better.

'November,' said Mum. 'That leaves six months.'
'I don't know what to do, Veronica.'
'You have to tell your parents, you must.'
'Oh God, I can't, Veronica. I can't.'
'You have to, you must. They'll find out soon enough.'
'Oh brother, if only you knew.'
Felicia and her big girlfriends were too big to speak to

James. Unless they wanted to beat him at jacks or send him to the shop for the latest edition of *Pop Hits*. Grace would never do that, even though she had twin brothers of her own, Everton and Clive. They said so in class.

'She's always being sick in the toilet,' they said last Friday whilst playing Snakes and Ladders.

Mum had stopped sighing by now but she was still looking worried.

'Who's the father?' asked Mum. And instead of answering the question Grace just looked down at the floor like she'd lost something. Grown-ups could do that, not answer questions and get away with it. If James or any of his friends or even Felicia didn't answer then they would be in big trouble. But grown-ups didn't have to, and even when they did, it didn't have to be right. And if the other grown-up didn't get the answer they wanted then they made one up for themselves.

'I know what you mean,' said Mum. 'When I was having Felicia I didn't say anything either. Oh boy, Mama went mad. And as for Aunt Vernice, well.'

Grace laughed, even though James couldn't see what was so funny. 'If only you knew,' she said. 'If only you knew.' And this time she laughed like she'd heard a really rude joke. Grown-ups were funny like that, laughing in the wrong places. Kids like James never had such problems. If something was funny, like Sooty, Basil Brush or Simon's jokes, then you laughed. If it wasn't funny then you didn't laugh – it was as simple as that. And no matter what anyone said, standing on the corner watching Mum and Grace talking to each other and looking really miserable was not funny at all. Simon was funny, Simon was always funny. No one could tell jokes as funny as Simon. Like the one about the boy who peed through a neighbour's letterbox then knocked on the door to find out how far the pee went. That one was funny.

'Trust me, girl, telling them would be the least of your problems.'

Grace shook her head again but this time she wasn't laughing. 'Oh brother. If only you knew, Veronica, if only you *knew*.'

Yes, thought James. One of Simon's jokes would do right now, they needed cheering up. A really rude joke, perhaps, with lots of poo noises and semolina pudding, so funny that snot would run down your nose and Mrs Ryan would send you to Mr Boyle for the slipper. The one about the vicar, perhaps, with the stripper and a box of Liquorice Allsorts.

Now that one was *really* funny.

four

'Coronation Street with Coloured People? Nice book title. There's one already? Well I'll be . . .'

If it was the beginning it would be like the beginning of *The Sound of Music*, you know, where the camera flew through the skies over mountains and snow-covered dales until it flew right down and almost hit Julie Andrews in the back of her head. It was a lot like that only this was not snow-covered mountains and the Moss Side skies were packed with smog-filled clouds. Apart from that it was much the same as the camera zoomed down through the clouds until a row of houses came into view. *Coronation Street* with coloured people, that was Cadogen Street. They weren't all coloured people though, a few of them were white like those ones at the end of the road but they didn't count. There was Jake, and Mavis his wife of course. There was also Aunty Mary too, but that was another story.

The camera stopped when it came to Number 37; the house with the FOR SALE sign over the front window. Then up the stairs and first door on the right, the one with strange noises coming from it. James was having another nightmare, he had also wet his bed again.

A dying soldier in a crater after a bomb or something. If you looked carefully you could see the mud and blood on his uniform. The soldier picked a poppy, it smelt nice. Over in the distance, weary soldiers marched back to base. Only they couldn't find it so they marched round in circles instead. Behind them was a trail of leftovers from the last battle: dead bodies, dead horses, even dead vehicles. And everything went deeper and deeper into the mud each time the soldiers went round. Over in the distance was the sound of singing and laughter. It was the triumphant army back at their own base. Someone had found dozens of cases of brown ale and ginger beer in one of the trenches.

Meanwhile, back in the crater, the soldier opened his eyes and yawned. Then he wiped his hand on his coat and rummaged in one of the top pockets and pulled out a sweet. A Mo-Jo.

'What's the capital of France? Dead easy. Spell Mississippi, even easier, M-I-doubles-I-doubles-I-doubleP-I, ta da! Go on, ask me another, anything, any subject you like. Who cut the Gordon knot, how many shillings in a guinea, what's eight times eight?'

James was used to the damp blankets by now, but not enough to stop the nightmares.

Lieutenant James looked through his other pockets but couldn't find any more Mo-Jos. It was always that way with sweets, whenever you wanted more there'd be no

more left and the way things were it would be a while before he could find a sweetshop.

'If there was a fire in the bed I'd be a hero and the Queen would give me a medal at Buckingham Palace, *with Alice*.'

A shell exploded over the top of the crater. Mud and dust went everywhere, including up Lieutenant James's nose.

'Who killed Cock Robin? It was I, said the Sparrow, with my bow and arrow.'

James looked down at his lap. It looked like a wet rag. As he looked closer, he felt the water running down his leg. The wet rag was a dead rat.

'Bungalow, B-U-N-G-A-L-O-W, loud applause, thank you thank you so much it was nothing really, where's that ringing coming from, someone's at the door, why don't no one answer, please someone answer, why don't it stop ringing, it might be a ghost, it must be a ghost, oh no it's **a DEAD RAT, ARRR!!**'

The alarm clock fell to the floor, still ringing even though James had given it a punch that would've knocked out Muhammad Ali. But as James looked out the window, it looked like a glorious sunny morning. It was a Tuesday schoolday morning so it had to be a glorious sunny morning to make it worth getting up. A Tuesday schoolday morning with only one bathroom and Laura was giving as good as she got if the screaming was anything to go by. And downstairs, Felicia was making the breakfast as well before catching the eight-thirty bus to Central High. All this because she passed her 11-plus. Mum was on her sewing machine making bras and girdles for Mr Mackenzie. She said she made peanuts too, but James didn't believe her. She also said she was an outdoor worker, but she was always in the front room, even at nights, making bras girdles and peanuts.

James hated cornflakes as well as Tuesday mornings even when glorious and sunny. If James had his way, there would be no school. Just dry nights and long summer Sundays playing football in the park and watching musicals on the telly. If he had his way, Tuesday mornings would **go something like this** . . .

'California Girls' by the Beach Boys accompanied by a breakfast of bacon eggs and tomatoes with toast and lashings of ginger beer. James gulps down his tea and Mum playfully pats him on the head, puts his school cap on and hands him his satchel. His sisters wave him goodbye and he waves back as he strides through the door. As he steps outside he starts to tap dance in time to the music. Errol and Roy join in and they add a shrug of the shoulders Jimmy Cagney style. Then one by one the neighbours join in until the whole street is full of tap dancing and shoulder shrugging, and it all ends when the introduction ends and the singing starts. Then everyone goes about their business like it was nothing special, and James and Errol and Roy go on to school. That was how it would be on the telly. But it wasn't the telly. It was just a gloriously sunny Tuesday morning and Tuesdays meant Spelling Test. James hated Spelling, even though he always came top. The others made fun of him.

Mum shouted over the droning of the machine, 'Hope you brought your blankets down, young man? Get a box of washing powder on your way back. Money's in me purse.'

She'd been up since seven and Dad was up even earlier

even though they'd both been up late last night after going to make sure things were okay at the brand new house in Ashton-under-Lyne with a front lawn, a garage and cherry tree at the front. So early it was dark, even in summer. Dad never talked about his job, he just returned every night so they could have dinner at seven-thirty exactly. Dad didn't know it but James had a special adventure for him as he returned from work, if he wanted it.

'Macartney's Park'. It was a great song, but the singer was rubbish. James would be chased by those big lads from Albermarle Street, all the way from Denmark Road where the old market used to be, past the brewery which stank of boiled turnips, past those Chad Valley high-rise flats, through Platt Fields Park where there was a fair every summer. Just as they were about to catch him and beat him up, Dad would jump out and stand in front of James, with hands on hips. The boys would run away because they were so scared of Dad. And instead of the guy singing, it would be Dad that did the singing. All the neighbours turn out to greet the conquering hero. And Dad would stand there, with arms akimbo, because akimbo meant hands on hips, Aunty Mary said.

And when he came to the end and sang

♪Oh No!!♪

all the neighbours would stand behind him with their arms in the air like *The Gang Show*. Then everyone would go indoors to finish off what they were doing before.

Splat! A spoonful of soggy cornflakes hit James in the face. A few moments later, James caught up with Errol and

Carl halfway down Broadfield Road.

'What you runnin' for?'

'Nothing.'

After Laura had thrown the cornflakes in his face, James had emptied his bowl over her head. And of course she'd started to cry. Cry would be an understatement. Bawl like she had both her eyes poked out and her fingernails pulled off would be more like it. When he tried to shut her up by throwing the tablecloth over her head, the milk jug spilt all over Felicia's *Pop Hits* magazine. James didn't hang around after that. In two seconds flat he'd put on his shoes, combed his hair, packed his school bag, taken half a crown from Mum's purse for the washing powder, and was halfway down Broadfield Road. Carl and Errol were not impressed.

'What do you mean nothing?'

'I said nothing, okay?'

Errol and Carl whispered to each other. Then without warning Errol grabbed James from the back. Errol was the Cock of the class so it was no use struggling. But that didn't stop him from kicking and screaming *geroff*. Carl grabbed one of James's legs. 'Poo,' he said, 'I can smell him from here. Told you he wet his bed again.'

'Geroff,' screamed James. 'Geroff!'

Errol and Carl laughed as they shook James like a raggedy doll. 'Wet your bed, wet your bed,' they chanted, like a football song at Maine Road and Manchester City were beating United one-nil. 'You can't go to Ashton if you wet your bed. Wet your bed, wet your bed . . .'

James gave up struggling and decided to let them shake until they got bored. Besides, it was too late now, it would be all round the class by ten o'clock and all round the school by dinner time, if Carl had his way. So there was no use in doing anything really except to try and keep his shoes and socks on. While he was at it why not take in the scenery? **Wasn't this the same street where he'd got the whole class to sing 'Holy Broken Bones'?**

♪**Holy broken bones, holy broke, holy broken bones ... ♪ to the tune of 'Good Vibrations' by the Beach Boys. They'd just had the Wednesday morning session at the local swimming pool. Wednesday meant Arithmetic Test as soon as they got back to school so everyone was dead miserable. James thought they needed cheering up. They sang all the way to the school gates.**

Dinner break, and playing jacks with Felicia and her big girlfriends because no one else would play with him. They'd had lunch. Chips and something. Anything with chips was his favourite, those being the days before you had chips with everything. It wasn't semolina or sago or rice pudding for pudding. He couldn't remember what it was, but he had seconds as usual. Felicia didn't give him a Chinese burn, thank goodness. All she did was twist his arm round his back until he screamed for mercy. James knew he was getting off lightly, so he didn't say anything else. It also helped having his mind on other things . . .

***'Live at the London Palladium'* in painted multi-coloured splodges and streaks over a big sheet of white paper. Fireworks in the sky with a few peeows and whizzbangs and a line of high-kicking long-legged ladies that made James feel all funny inside. It was amazing what you could do with red and green paint mixed together with spit and a handful of Katie's hair. There used to be a whole Tuesday afternoon of painting when James was in the infants. Overalls were compulsory**

or else you'd be in a right mess. And if Mrs Rowbottom liked your picture, she would pin it to the wall with three stars for everyone to see. But none of James's creations ever made it that far.

'What's it meant to be, James?'

Now James was in the juniors and no one would sit with him because Carl told the whole class about him wetting his bed again. So now he was copying pictures of Cecil Rhodes and William the Bruce with tracing paper and writing about them all around the picture like *This Is Your Life*. Not as fun as painting but it was fun enough to make the mind wander all over the place and forget about the hard wooden stools and desks with holes for ink-wells that were never there; not as fun as painting but fun enough to wander off into another world, any world would do as long as it was far enough away from the stares, nudges, giggles and chair shuffles as the others tried to get away from him as far as possible.

'They don't let smellies into Ashton-under-Lyne.'

The world where he was right now was just perfect, thank you very much, **because it was a hot summer's morning with everyone on their way to church. The ladies in the wide-brimmed flowered hats and the men in their best Sunday suits and stiff collars, clutching leathered Bibles and sealed envelopes for the collection plate. Little boys in their smaller suits, bri-nylon shirts and elastic ties. And the girls in their bridesmaids dresses and pink handbags. Then it must be 'Oh Happy Day' by the Edwin Hawkins Singers.**

♪**When Jesus swore, it take your pants away**♪

Zoom up to the skies then look down, and it was a street out of Busby Berkeley, only they weren't dancing or they'd be late and miss the first hymn.

The school bell went clang. Home time, hurrah. A hot sunny Tuesday afternoon accompanied by the sound of a thousand feet tip tapping away from school as fast as possible. James joined them in perfect step even though he didn't do tap-dancing classes with his sisters. And none of them said anything because Carl hadn't spoken to them yet. But there was still a long way to go and anything could happen on those mean streets on the long trek home.

Three doorsteps to the right at Number 33 were two pints of milk, a bottle of orange and a dozen eggs. Three young boys round the corner. They'd seen the goodies and were waiting for the right moment to pounce. They'd be there for a long time if Mrs Smith had her way. She'd had an eye on them for ages now and was waiting for just the right moment to chuck a bucket of freezing cold water over those lazy good-for-nothing layabouts.

There was Charlie dressed up as a woman as usual. A bright yellow wig and a face with deep red lips and far too much mascara. A pink fluffy jacket, tight red mini-skirt and black stockings with high heels. He looked a right mess.

'Third Finger, Left Hand' by Martha Reeves and the Vandellas. Charlie would be pleased with that one; that and anything by Jim Reeves.

James had finally made it to the safety of home and changed into his playing clothes after having a wash. Mr Boyle had suggested he did so when he got home, immediately. And now, while Mum was sewing away, he was in the front hunched up on the window sill, nose pressed against the steamed-up window pane, with Mum not speaking to him because he forgot to buy the washing powder and the shops shut early on Tuesday. 'What am I going to do?' she said to the wall because she still wasn't speaking to him. It was raining outside, colouring everything to a damp dank grey. But James had done this one many times so he was ready for a change, but he couldn't decide where to. Another plane crash perhaps. Or maybe a night full of falling stars which were so bright the street lamps could be left off to save electricity. But as usual things sorted themselves out and **suddenly it was the annual church outing to Heaton Park – bring your own packed lunch and pop – a shilling for members of the choir; everyone else two bob. But now it was only a dream. One of those, you know, that you don't want to wake up from especially on those cold mornings when you have to take the blankets downstairs. James had got lost from everyone else. His friends were on the large front lawn terrorising the snogging students from Manchester University. Reverend Weiland was seated with the other elders, eating their cellophane lunches of cottage cheese, watercress and Ryvita crispbread.**

Even though he was lost, James was happy. It was the first deer he had ever seen. Or maybe it was a unicorn, a baby one at least. Just like Bambi. It stared at him with runny black eyes and a snotty nose, and it smelt like next-door's dog. When James touched its nose with his fingers it didn't run away. It just stood there chewing like it was a pet or something. He hadn't meant to get lost. He just wanted to get away from the others because they had nicked his butties. It took all his effort to hold on to the pork pie and can of Coke. He'd even said the F-word. Mum would've gone mad if she'd heard him say the F-word. Saying the F-word was much worse than forgetting to buy the washing powder for Tuesday wash night. Much worse, but not by that much.

He was glad they weren't here right now. They'd throw stones or something like that and spoil everything. They wouldn't appreciate the beautiful view either. A cartoon kaleidoscope of the whole of Manchester with a big red balloon of a sun so close you could warm your bum.

The front doorbell rang. James rushed to the front door and there she was. The lady from the soap powder advert on the telly. A really big blast from the trumpets so loud James almost fell over. A brand sparkling new blonde wearing an air-hostess dress with blue stockings and stilettos, grinning away like her dentures had stuck. In her right hand was a box of washing powder and in her left was a sheet of paper. The questions to win a free holiday or five pounds, just like off the telly.

'Mum!? Mum!!!'

You had to shout twice when Mum was sewing. Her slippers flip flopped on the linoed entrance as she came to the front door.

'It's the lady off the telly,' said James.

The fan of pound notes in the lady's right hand was of no interest to James or Mum, they only had eyes for that box of washing powder in her left hand, and when the lady-off-the-telly asked Mum if she had a box just like this, Mum said, 'No, but I'll buy it off you. The washhouse starts in five minutes.'

So the lady-off-the-telly gave Mum the box of washing powder as well as the five pounds because she knew Mum wouldn't know the answers. Then the lady-off-the-telly ran back to the car that was shaped like the box of powder and drove off really quickly because she had to be on the telly later that night. Mum was so pleased she put the money in the saving-up jar for a washing machine for their brand new house with a garage and a shared drive because there were no wash-houses in Ashton-under-Lyne.

'There's no Jamaicans there either,' Mum said.

The sun had gone down by now. With the night time you didn't have to try too hard as everything had a life of its own in the moonlight, and what were tatty and moth-eaten front room curtains during the day **became a battlefield of fire-eating dragons for St George to slay and Rapunzel to be rescued from the Leaning Tower of Pisa. Or if you didn't feel like it, you could leave things as they were, just change the day. So instead of a normal schoolday evening and in bed by nine o'clock, it was Saturday night at Aunty Vernice's. The smell of soiled bed clothes, boiled eggs and cod-liver oil. Rickety old banisters that should collapse any minute but didn't. Dark damp cellars the colour of coal. A kitchen the size of a shoe box but big enough to fry fish for five thousand. A grand old house of five floors, an attic and a million and one stairs. There was always a bus load of people every time James visited his Aunty Vernice. Felicia would be upstairs playing records with Clarence Harriet Deniece Benjamin and Colleen and Laura would be at home in bed. Radio Luxembourg would be on the radio and with James singing along like there was no tomorrow.**

♪I smiled for a while na na na, na na na na melancholy. Na na na na na milkshake while I caa ... aha ... an.♪

But it was school tomorrow, and Mum had returned from the wash-house hours ago. The bedroom coal-fire was lit because it was dead cold **outside so the little fire people ran in and out of the red-hot charcoal house to light up the skies with Standard fireworks.** It had been a long tiring Tuesday so James was fast asleep by now, with his fingers crossed and the plastic sheet ready. But it would be okay because he was having his favourite dream, **the one which always had a dry bed in the morning. The one with Mr Hagen, the estate agent in town. It began with him and Mum in Mr Hagen's office. He'd had good news. 'It's a five-year-old semi with three bedrooms, a kitchen hatch, separate bathroom and toilet, front and back gardens and shared drive ...'**

five

'Monster and dragon in Cadogen Street? You watch too much telly, young man.'

Cadogen Street had a strange look to it as day turned to dark. The red-bricked walls became endless hiding places for all sorts of monsters and dragons, and the tarmac road became a moonlit river of silver trout with marbled pavements along the side.

'How long did you say?' asked Mr Williams.

'Won't be long now,' said James.

Mrs Smith and Mrs Jones were there too, sat on the settee from James's house. He had promised to make them feel comfortable or else they wouldn't have come. There was no problem with Mr Williams though. Ever since James saw him with a white lady in a short skirt in the back alley last Thursday Mr Williams had been ever so nice. He even gave James a ten bob note just to keep quiet which was easy really as James hadn't recognised the lady as anyone from around there anyway.

James was nervous though. It usually happened on time but what if it didn't? Then they would call him a liar and Mrs Smith and Jones would tell Mum and Mr Williams wouldn't give him any more ten bob notes.

'If you're telling lies, boy.'

'I'm not Mrs Jones, honest. Won't be long now, honest.'

He needn't have worried because at that very moment a drum roll began and the moon shone a spotlight on James like he was the star of the London Palladium show. 'Not me, stupid, over there!'

The spotlight swung over to the front door of Number 22, Grace Jackson's house, which by now was giving its very own show. Shouting and screaming followed by the slamming of doors rounded off by all the lights flashing on and off like they couldn't decide whose turn it was. Mrs Smith and Jones showed their appreciation by clapping till their hands hurt. Mr Williams wasn't too keen though; he sat there and sulked.

Suddenly everything stopped. No lights, no screaming, no banging, not even no drum roll. Nothing. For about a minute, though, it seemed a lot longer.

'I think he's gone too far this time,' said Mrs Smith, crocheting yet another doily mat for the mantelpiece.

'Hope not,' replied Mrs Jones. 'She owes me two bob, does Grace.'

Mr Williams couldn't wait any longer, the tension was too much. 'Damn girl asks for it anyway,' he said as he stood up, this time remembering to take his chair back with him. But he had to sit down again when things at Number 22 started up again. And sure enough, a whimpering sound came from the upstairs front bedroom even though the curtains were closed. And if they listened carefully, they could hear the clanking of dishes and taps running.

'For a moment there I was really worried,' said Mrs Smith.

'Don't matter,' replied Mrs Jones, 'she paid me back yesterday.'

Cadogen Street had a strange look to it as day turned to dark. The monsters and dragons in the walls had fallen asleep by now and the moonlit river of silver trout had finally come to rest. The others had gone back indoors, only James was outside and he wasn't going anywhere. Not until the sobbing stopped.

six

'Maybe a pantomime wasn't such a bad idea after all.'

He'd thought of telling the truth, you know, that a little girl had stolen the money from his shopping bag. But that wouldn't do no good. Mum would beat him anyway for being so stupid.

When James was a baby in the hospital he wouldn't cry with the other babies. If they started, he would stop, and vice versa, Mum said. Every Christmas Mum told that one, and Easter, and Whitsuntide. Whenever there was a roomful of people and the telly was off.

When James was a toddler he had a special glass, and whenever Dad or any grown-ups opened a bottle of beer he would run to the kitchen cupboard to collect his little glass and run back before they'd drunk the whole bottle. Then he would hold it out like he was Oliver Twist. They laughed of course, maybe called him names and pretend to be vexed. And after saying thank you very much, James would go into his special chair and sip slowly, so it would last as long as possible, Mum said. James didn't remember any of this. Neither did he recall when he ate a loaf of bread with no butter or margarine. He didn't say a word the whole time. He just chewed away until the whole loaf was gone, Dad said. He was also a toddler when Mum would tie him to a lamp-post, but that didn't stop him running away. She only knew something was wrong when a smiling policeman with James on his shoulder knocked on the door.

'Does this one belong to you?'

'I don't remember any of this,' he said, but they never believed him. They laughed and told him to go about his business. They wouldn't believe him now, either. They would say he had stolen the money and spent it on ice-cream or comics or something.

James was older, but younger than he was now, when he saw Robert Kennedy being shot. It was lunchtime. He was at home from school eating fish and chips, when suddenly there was a bang on the telly and Robert Kennedy fell to the ground with his eyes wide open. James had been having lunch at home ever since his friends had given him the smallest portion of meat pie from the tray at the end of the table. Afterwards they said it was a joke, but James would have none of it and when Mum said yes you can come home for lunch, James was so happy he punched Carl in the face. It was a good job too or else he would never have seen Robert Kennedy being shot on the midday news by a man with a funny name.

There was no need to tell anyone about that one, Christmas, Easter or Whitsuntide, no need whatsoever. He was a big boy now, not a baby or toddler. And big boys didn't cry neither, even if they wanted to.

It would be more than shame when he got home. Never

mind what Mum would do. What about Dad? Was it only that evening that all he had to worry about was what time the ice-cream van was coming and whether there were enough pennies for a cornet or an ice-lolly? Before Mum had told him to go get some bread and milk, butter and cornflakes and ruined his life forever and ever amen. They would kill him when he got home. They'd break his body into little bits and put them into one of the big boxes in the entrance that was there to pack stuff away in. He'd be lucky if he was allowed to watch telly ever again. A life without telly was a life not worth living. They might just as well shoot him in the head. Or make him drink gallons of castor oil and eat a dozen Marmite sandwiches washed down by a bucket of cold Bovril. Not that it would bother them. Mum and Dad said there was no telly back *home*; all they had in the evenings was a night full of fireflies and stars falling from the skies with a chorus of crickets, bullfrogs and the local steel band playing 'St Kitts at Night'. And if they were really lucky the church hall would show the latest Errol Flynn film again, even though the white blanket had a hole in the middle.

James hoped the girl who stole his money had no telly. She was scruffy enough to have no telly, buttons missing from her duffel coat, greasy hair down to her shoulder, a pale face that needed feeding. She smelt too. But that was the last thing on his mind when he first saw her. He thought she was being friendly when she came up to him and said, 'Hello.'

This wasn't the time for shimmering streets and terraces of fruit pastilles. Cadogen Street was just a sign with a tarmac road down the middle and houses on both sides. Some had lights on, some didn't. Others had windows boarded up and the one on the corner had a red light. Any minute now it would be so dark you couldn't see anything, so it wouldn't matter if he stepped in some dog muck and scraped his shoes all over the carpet. It wouldn't matter because he'd be dead as soon as he got in. They'd know the truth right away because it was written all over his face in big print letters.

James kicked an old tin can into the middle of the road. Normally it would be a goal and the crowd would go mad. But they didn't because they could read too. It was still written all over his face.

'You let a little girl steal the money, stupid.'

James stopped suddenly as he came to the crossroads between Monton Road and Moss Lane East by the zebra crossing. The same zebra crossing where he had crossed without permission and all the cars and lorries had to stop with a screech; the same zebra crossing where the policeman had smacked him on the bum and called him a stupid boy; the same zebra crossing which had led on to Monton Road then Normanby Street then home to Cadogen Street that Tuesday afternoon for a lunch-break of egg and chips and tomato ketchup. When Mum had asked James what was the matter, he burst into tears and couldn't stop crying, even after Mum went to school to tell the teacher James was too ill for school that afternoon even though it was games. It was only a little smack. He'd had much worse than that from Mr Boyle's slipper. But the policeman wasn't a teacher, nor his Mum or Dad, and only they could hit him like that. Not a policeman.

All of a sudden things didn't seem so bad after all. It wasn't as if there was any policeman about, not at that time of night anyway. And as Aunty Mary would say, 'It's not like anyone's died.'

So with a hop, skip and a jump the skies came to life, a multicoloured extravaganza of pink, green and sticky back plastic. The houses became a terrace of Cadbury's milk chocolate with sugar-coated windows and candy floss curtains. He'd better run, get it over and done with. Hopefully it would be Dad that did the beating and not Mum. Mum would use anything close by, such as a broomstick or the big soup pot, whereas Dad was a good old-fashioned belt man. James would cry, of course. You had to with Dad, or else he wouldn't stop. He must remember not to say *I'm sorry Dad I won't do it again*, because that was asking for trouble.

'I ... iii ... II ... geeeve ... yooouuu ... sommme ... thhhiing ... toooo ... beeeeeee ... sorrrryyyyy ... aaaaa ... bbbbb ... oooouuuu ... ttttttt ...' with a slap for each letter and full stop. He wouldn't be able to sit down for ages neither. He'd have to wash the dishes for a week and miss pocket money too. Laura and Felicia would laugh, of course, and Mum wouldn't speak to him, and Rose wouldn't know any better because she was just a toddler. And as Aunty Mary would say, 'Worse things happen at sea.'

seven

'What's a Kilroy, Aunty Mary?'

Only last week it had been a row of houses. Fairlawn Street next to St Bees Street next to another road James couldn't remember the name of. Each house had three floors and a million stairs to the top. Only last week the streets were full of kids playing catch and cars driving past the women gossiping on the corner. But not any more, all that was gone and all that was left was a pool the size of a school yard and a reflection of the church spire. The church was the only building left, apart from the pub at the end of what used to be St Bees Street. The pub had a large poster of a man and woman smiling up to the skies like they'd seen a bird. If they'd been looking to the ground they wouldn't be smiling. Who would when all that was left was a big pool the size of a school yard. It was like the 'blitts' as Aunty Mary called it, like a bomb had exploded and all the houses disappeared in a puff of smoke and a loud bang. A lot of things happened during the 'blitts', said Aunty Mary. Fernleaf Street died in one night. Hitler did it, said Aunty Mary. It couldn't be Hitler's fault this time. James had seen the men with bulldozers, in their white hats and muddy boots. There wasn't a short man with a moustache amongst them.

Just think, only last week James had been playing football with Gary and Eugene against the cornershop wall with painted-on goal posts and *Kilroy was here*. But now everything was gone and James had to be careful of stepping in the mud as he was wearing his trousers after Wednesday choir practice and if he got mud on his trousers again Mum would kill him, again.

The reflection of the church spire in the water was so big it was like a twin brother, in the pool the size of a school yard which was once Fairlawn Street, St Bees Street and another road whose name James couldn't remember. It was like the pool was saying sorry for letting all those houses be knocked down. But it was too late now, and no amount of pictures in the pool would bring any of it back.

A doll's head, a mud-caked shoe and a broken down pram, right in the middle of the big pool. And there next to the reflection of the church spire was a post with a HALT sign with a triangle in a circle. A bit like a lollipop man's pole only this one had black and white stripes and was stuck in the ground. That was all that was left from what used to be the street where Mum stayed for the first night she arrived in England after spending three weeks on a ship called *The Canary*. The men in the white hats and muddy boots did a pretty good job, apart from the doll's head and the black and white pole with a HALT sign. Maybe they'd forgotten about them, the men in the muddy boots. Maybe they felt sorry and decided to let them stay and live happily ever after. The post had its own reflection like the church spire and the midday sun. But that wouldn't last. As soon as it was summer then even the pool would go away and the HALT sign would be left on its own, along with the doll's head, the mud-caked shoe and the broken down pram.

It was like the end of the world as we know it. And if it was the end of the world there'd be no more school or telly and it would be so cold you'd have to wear your overcoat, vest and two pairs of underpants. If it was the end of the world there'd be no need to brush your teeth or comb your hair every day. There would be no semolina pudding and no matter how many times you counted to a zillion there'd be no one left to play hide and seek.

If it was the end of the world. But it wasn't. Even so, James didn't want to think of it no more as it made him sad and he wanted to get home quick as soon as possible. Anywhere there were people in the street, children playing break the window with a football, clothes hung out on washing lines across the street like a carnival parade, dogs cocking their legs and watering lamp-posts. Yes, he wanted to get home as soon as possible but he had to be very careful indeed as he was still in his Sunday best and he was stuck in the middle of the pool the size of a school yard. If he was really careful and hopscotched his way along all the dry spots, with a bit of luck he would only have a bit of mud on the turn-ups and that was easy to get rid of. The tap in the backyard should do the trick. But even if he was caught he wouldn't mind getting into trouble and having to stay in for a whole week. And having to wash the dishes every night, going to bed early even though it was the holidays, to a bedroom with two bunks and a fireplace that was lit on cold winter nights when the taps would freeze all night and it would be all right in the morning because the sun would come out and melt the cold away, and the taps and the bedroom and the house and Rose Laura Felicia Mum and Dad would still be there long after the sun had melted the pool which was once Fairlawn Street, St Bees Street and another road James couldn't remember the name of, down to the size of a peanut.

eight

'You can choose your family but you can't choose your friends. No, that's not right.'

It was dead easy really, dead easy to play Cowboys and Indians in Mum's sewing room. Or rocket to the moon, or be kidnapped by pirates on the Caribbean Sea. Everything was there already, especially when Mr Mackenzie had a big order on. Then there'd be a big box of stocking clips which made ideal cavalrymen. And the bendy metal straps that went into bras to stop them flopping down made excellent Indian headgear when ten of them were stuck into Laura's hair. That was why she didn't mind being an Indian, she loved having the bendy metal straps sticking out of her hair, as long as she put them in herself. The foam from the bra cups could be anything from a row of Indian tee-pees to a helmet in case you changed your mind and wanted to play spaceships instead. Laura didn't mind either way. Just as long as she could keep the metal bands in her hair.

Sometimes, if Mum was low on stuff and Mr Mackenzie hadn't delivered for a while, she'd shout at them to put everything back *I won't tell you again*. But most of the time she was content to let them play as they wanted because at least she could keep an eye on James and know he wasn't getting into any mischief. Not that she minded him playing with the big boys. But lately he'd wanted to stay in a lot more and when she asked what was up he said nothing Mother, and she thought that was strange he's never called me Mother before, and when he asked when were they moving house she thought that was strange too because he already knew when so there was no need to ask. But that was the way things were lately, so when she said he could only stay in if he promised to look after Laura and he said okay straight away she wasn't the least bit surprised.

Yes, it was dead easy to play Cowboys and Indians but to be perfectly frank as Aunty Mary would say, 'I've had enough of them to last me a lifetime.' Something else was needed, something just right.

'It has to be just right,' said James aloud to himself as no one else was listening. A plush lush sound, you know, Nelson Riddle with Frank Sinatra and Ella Fitzgerald. Nat King Cole would be there too but he couldn't because he was dead. On the count of three, one two three . . . **James knew the next bit almost by heart having done it so many times. The street flowed down to a shimmering haze, the houses became a row of fruit pastilles, blah blah blah. The last time was when he got all those balls back from Mr Price, the phantom ball catcher of Albermarle Street. Millions of them splashed out on to the street. Big ones, small ones, all different colours of the rainbow ones, rounded off with a double twist ninety-nine with** strawberry chocolate syrup nuts and hundreds and thousands. Not today though, he wasn't hungry.

'I feel like dancing,' said James. So he sent the violins away and put on a record instead.

'It's "Madison Time",' said the man on the record. And as if by magic, all the neighbours were out and lined up in rows like school assembly. Only they weren't singing hymns or saying the Lord's Prayer. They were dancing instead. A side-stepping, finger-clicking, hip-on-roller-skates formation as only coloured people on Cadogen Street can. James rushed out to join in. 'Perfect!'

Everyone was out there. Mr and Mrs Bruce with all their eight children. Even Patricia, though she was meant to be doing her homework. Mrs Green by herself as Mr Green was on night shift. James had never seen Mr Green, ever. He wondered if Mrs Green was making him up. Even those white people from the end of the road that didn't speak to nobody but themselves were there. They couldn't do the hips-on-roller-skates bit of course, but they clicked their fingers in the right places. Old Jake was there, with the wooden leg he got in the war. He was wearing a cap too. Mum, Dad, Felicia and Laura had joined them by now. Their only concern was to look as cool as everyone else. And when the music changed key, not one of them missed a beat. They even did a hop, skip, turnaround just to prove the point.

Suddenly there was a tap on his shoulder. Grace Jackson from across the road, a grown-up even though she lived with her parents. She was wearing a red outdoor coat with a fur collar and was carrying a battered old suitcase. 'Can you turn the volume up? It'll give me more time.'

'Okay,' shrugged James. They were dancing well

enough, but if that was what she wanted. Grace thanked him even though she seemed far away. The neighbours were still dancing, but something was different. The same music, steps and everything, but it wasn't happy any more. Then he saw Mr and Mrs Jackson. They were dancing with everyone else, but that was all. Mr Jackson's lips were bleeding and there were scratch marks all down his face. And Mrs Jackson was staring at her slippers like their laces were undone. James looked up at Grace. Her lips were bleeding too and some plaits had been pulled out. Strange, he hadn't noticed the bulge on her stomach before. You couldn't miss it now. Not even under the coat and flowery white night-dress. James had an idea, it came to him like a flash.

'Next time,' said James, 'next time they'll all have top hat and tails, just like Fred Astaire.'

Grace was crying now, tears rolled down her face, mixing with the blood and spit before falling to the ground.

'Keep it going for a bit longer will you.'

And with that she picked up her suitcase, walked around the corner and disappeared for ever. Mr Jackson looked like he wanted to tell her to get inside before he took his belt off to her. As for Mrs Jackson, her laces were still undone. And as for everyone else, they had seen it all before. If it wasn't Grace it was something else. It was none of their business anyway. Besides, they were dancing.

A few minutes later and everything was over. All the neighbours were back indoors and Cadogen Street was left clear for night time to take over. Dad was in bed, Mum was washing the dishes and James was finishing off Dad's leftover chicken leg from this evening's dinner. It was always like this after a row. The same row from Aunty Vernice's party last week. Aunty came on her usual afternoon visit, only this time she didn't bring any ice-cream. It ended when Aunty Vernice stormed out of the house like she'd finally won the pools, but not before she bumped into one of the boxes in the entrance, the one with all the old curtains and clothes from the old wardrobe in the coal cellar. And when Dad went to see Mum in the kitchen she screamed at him to get the hell out of there and he did too, he didn't hit her neither. He just left her and returned to his chair to watch Sunday league cricket on the telly. Mum also threw a pot of rice at him before he left the kitchen and Felicia had to clear up the mess. No one said a word at the table and Dad left most of the dinner, including the chicken leg, and went straight to bed. Mum and Felicia had an argument too. Not the same as with Dad, but it was just as loud. This one also ended with Felicia going to bed. Only this time Mum sent her. And now Mum was washing the dishes in the kitchen. She sang hymns too. She always sang hymns when she was upset, even when it wasn't a Sunday.

Grace hadn't said goodbye to anyone, not even Mum. She wasn't dressed properly neither, people would laugh at her when they saw her like that. When they did move to Ashton-under-Lyne James would make sure he said goodbye to everyone. All his friends at school, everyone at church, next door's dog, even those white people down the road.

nine

'No, I won't sing *"Tammy"*, Aunty Mary. You can't make me.'

It had been on the telly the night before, the *Nine O'Clock News*, the sinking of the *Christina*. Usually James was in bed by then, but Dad let him stay up. He normally hated the news and horse racing on ITV. But last night was different. It was the first time anything from *home* had been on the telly. But now it was Sunday after church and Mum had other things on her mind.

'I can't make me mind up with you young man, are you stupid or what?'

The tear on his trousers was bigger, from the bottom of the zip to the back pocket. A bit more and there'd be two halves to his Sunday best trousers.

'I must have said a million times to take them off straight away...'

But James knew her heart wasn't in it. Besides, it was worth getting your pants ripped just to see the expression on Errol's face. He would've got clean away if he hadn't stopped to laugh. It was so funny, Errol's face after James had kicked him between the legs.

'It was him that started it. He was making fun of me, about us moving house. Mum, what's a snob?'

The rules of the game were quite simple. One goalie and one goal – painted posts on the wall at the corner of Normanby Street. And as many players as you liked, no more than five or else it turned into a rugby match. It started off simple enough. Carl shouted:

'Pass the flippin' ball will *yor*.'

And James did. A nutmeg through Errol's big fat legs. Errol tried to elbow James in the face. James had known Errol since the infants, so later when the others said it was a good job you ducked or else you'd be in hospital with a broken head, James could say with all modesty:

'It was nothing really.'

The rest should've been even simpler. A sunny Sunday afternoon after church with a freshly nicked ball from the newsagents. But nothing was ever that simple for James, not lately anyway. **First of all there was Debbie Reynolds singing ♪Tammy♪ to contend with. Over and over again, like the record had stuck. Not as bad as Mum singing hymns but not far off.** Good job no one else could hear it. Boy would they laugh. It was totally inappropriate for the situation, this being the FA League Anglo-Italian Watneys Cup Final and all.

Then there was that other thing. It was the first time anything from home had been on the telly. But it looked no different to anything else. All they showed was a map of St Kitts with some arrows on it. Dad kept on saying 'Lord have mercy' and Mum went pale.

But first things first, Tammy.

♪The peas in the basin keeps murdering low, Tammy, Tammy's in lerve♪

This was worse than the theme from 'White Horse' that Felicia and her big girlfriends sang all daft and girlie like. And anything by Johnny Mathis or Engelbert Humperdinck. It was even worse than a Sunday afternoon matinée with Deanna Durbin prancing around in a white frilly skirt singing, 'La la la la la la laaaa.'

He tried a lunging tackle but missed and scraped his knees on the tarmac.

'Arr, me knee.'

And if what happened next had happened to anyone else they would've been really surprised. They'd have said flipping heck or goodness gracious me or even the F-word. But it didn't happen to anyone else, it happened to James and he had stopped being surprised a long time ago. One minute he was rolling holding his knee like it was broken in half, watching the others continue to play ignoring his distress. **The next he was shouting, 'Grab me leg,' to a big fat lady as he tried to clamber on board a lifeboat. The others were behaving just as stupid, like they wanted to drown. They were either screaming or fighting with each other and some just sat there crying or staring out to sea as if waiting for an answer from Sir.**

Mum was not pleased when cleaning his knee later on. 'You goner have to let it bleed. I've run out of Band Aid,' as she smeared on some TCP. But James could tell her heart wasn't in it.

'Grab me leg,' he said, even though he couldn't swim. He could really, but only in Broadfield Road Baths, and with arm floats and a plastic board. It didn't matter anyway as the man in the white suit wasn't having much

luck either. James was puzzled though. Apart from the screaming and shouting and people jumping overboard, everything seemed all right. The ferry was going along just fine. The sea was calm too, as flat as a pancake. Nevis was getting nearer by the minute, in a quarter of an hour it would've docked and everyone could've got off safely enough. But according to Richard Baker on the *Nine O'Clock News* this was not to be.

The news report said there had been too many passengers on board as it was a bank holiday and there was a carnival in Nevis. But for the people on board the carnival was over even before it started. Richard Baker said more than two hundred people drowned and they were still counting. One of them was Dad's Cousin Alma, they found out later. There was an old black and white wedding picture of her and her husband in the photo album. She was almost twice his size, and twice as wide. Her dark bright eyes stared out of the polythene cover like she was daring anyone to answer back. **James didn't remember seeing her on the boat though. He'd been rudely interrupted by** Errol charging straight at him.

'Get out of the way, snob. I'm Jairzinio, I'm goner score the greatest goal ever, you snob, get out of my way.'

James had to act fast or else he'd be smashed to smithereens. As Errol took aim with his right foot – and it wasn't the football he was aiming for – James did a little side step and slid the ball right from under his feet. There wasn't much time to celebrate. As Errol lunged feet-first at James with the intention of breaking every bone in James's body, James did a swivel of the hips, flicked the ball over his head with his right foot and simultaneously and at the same time kicked Errol in between the legs. Then, in the same breath, with only the goalie, a Ford Zephyr and Debbie Reynolds to beat, James took aim and fired! Just inside the bottom left-hand corner post. The ball left a dirt mark so there could be no argument whatsoever. Brian hadn't stood a chance in goal. No way could he have saved that one, even if he tried.

Errol had stopped screaming by now, but he was still writhing on the floor and whimpering like a big baby. James strode forward in slow motion to replace the awestruck Brian in goal. The others were just as gobsmacked. Even so, there was no way they would be in James's shoes. Not for a million pounds, or even a snog with Raquel Welch. All that remained was a warm glow and another tune. This one being more suitable for the mess he was in. That was how to get home alive, and in one piece.

'Mission: Impossible!'

It had been on the telly the night before, the *Nine O'Clock News*, the sinking of the *Christina* as it sailed from St Kitts to Nevis. They showed a map of St Kitts with some arrows on it. But that didn't matter. Dad kept on saying 'Lord have mercy,' and Mum went pale. Then some of Dad's friends came round as they didn't have a telly. After the news they sat round shaking their heads saying 'Lord have mercy,' too. And they didn't leave until after midnight because someone else came round who knew someone else who had a phone that could get to the West Indies. James could hear them through the bedroom floor. It was just like Christmas Eve, only they weren't wrapping presents.

ten

'What is it with you and plane crashes, James? It's morbid if you ask me.'

It was exactly as James had imagined it would be in the West Indies. A long dark path surrounded by trees and bushes so dense they hid the morning sun, the ground as soft as a warm blanket, the air smelling of freshly baked bread, cinnamon, raisins and cow dung, and everything was all snug and comfy cosy like in Mum's and Dad's bedroom where you'd rushed to after waking up screaming. A cricket chirped in the background followed by another and then another. Other animals and insects joined in until eventually there was a wonderful chorus of sounds and scents. And all this under a night full of stars. James had picked a ripe mango from one of the bushes along the path. It was nothing like the shrivelled up ones from Mr Singh's corner shop. These were so big and bulging their branches almost touched the ground. Juices oozed from their skins like fat men in tight vests so that any moment they would drop and splat to the ground so that the ants and flies would think it was Christmas.

With mango juice all over his face and hands, the chorus of the crickets and other insects, and enough fruit to last for a lifetime, James would've easily stayed there for ever and ever, amen. And he would've too if he hadn't seen the woman on the other side of the path. She wore a robe round her body like she was an African even though Dad said there were no Africans left in the West Indies. She beckoned him to come over like she had something nice to give him.

'Come here little boy.'

For a nine-year-old, James had seen a great deal. A plane crash into Greenheys School. Miss Young's knickers and suspenders as she bent down to pick up the chalk Errol had thrown under her desk. Batman, Robin and all the Supervillains on Princess Road. James had seen a great deal but it was the first time he had ever been in a truck full of people, even in the West Indies. The truck was on the morning run taking the workers to the cane fields in Sandy Point. The woman had given him exact instructions.

'Don't say nothing to no one. And if any policeman stops you, you don't know nothing about no rum, okay?' That was how he came to know it was bottles of rum in the bag. The woman had told him to take the bag to a man with a pipe who would be waiting in the field with a pile of sugar-cane in the middle.

'Don't forget the money, six dollar. Don't you come back without it neither or I'll cut your backside.'

Grown-ups were like that when they wanted you to do something bad for them. Like Uncle Luke telling you to go to the corner shop for a pack of Woodbines. Or the strange man in the Ford Cortina offering you some pear drops.

'I know you're not to speak to strangers but I won't say nothing if you won't. Maybe you prefer Liquorice Allsorts ... hey come back.'

However, as the truck bounced along the narrow lanes, James had more immediate problems. One of the bottles was leaking.

The woman had forgotten to say that the man who he was meant to meet had no teeth, only a little black stub in the middle of his top gums. She'd also forgotten to mention his blood-stained shirt and the big knife the size of an axe.

'Want some soup, boy?'

At times like this the worst thing to do was run like hell.

'Don't run, don't even look scared. He won't bark after that, you'll see,' Dad said after James had been chased by the big Alsatian at Number 10.

'Take some soup?'

This wasn't no Campbell's tomato chicken oxtail or minestrone soup either. This was soup eaten by every family from back home in Moss Side Manchester in the late sixties. Yams, sweet potatoes, dumplings, pumpkin, green bananas, Tania, plantain, okra and a piece of meat on a gigantic bone which you sucked the marrow from because it made your teeth strong. Normally James would pretend he was sick or throw spoonfuls of it behind the kitchen sink when no one was looking. But now wasn't normal and the big knife was close to the man's hand. Besides, with chunks of bread and a cup full of the rum, somehow the bowl of soup seemed just right. James held out his bowl.

'Can I have some more please?'

'Albert, me name Albert, Albert Redding.'

'Can I have some more, Albert. Please?'

Albert Redding, one of the sugar-cane choppers on the estate. Albert Redding, the same Albert Redding that chopped up two boys with a machete, Mum said. And when they caught him he was sent away to Trinidad because the prison in St Kitts only had one cell and that was being used already. James had guessed he was Albert Redding even before he said. The blood-stained shirt had given it away. And as he chomped away at another piece of sweet potato, James came to the conclusion that the boys must have looked scared or maybe they didn't like soup or else Albert would not have done what he did. There was one last piece of meat in the pot and if Albert didn't want it then why let good food go to waste? And as James made a whistle sound as he sucked the marrow from a bone he thought of the woman who'd given him the rum for Albert. There was something else he was supposed to do but no matter how hard he tried he could not remember. Maybe some more rum would help him to remember. So James held out his cup.

And as Albert poured more rum into his cup, James suddenly remembered something strange about the woman which had puzzled him at the time.

One of her fingers was missing.

eleven

'Miss Young wasn't your favourite teacher, was she.'

'Popeye the Sailor Man' over and over again, round and round the playground. They must have been round a million times even though playtime was only five minutes old. 'Popeye the Sailor Man'.

Errol was at the front leading everyone like it was him that wrote the words. James just sat by the wall by the railings. He wasn't going to join in even though he knew the words off by heart. He could see everything they did wrong. Cynthia and Maureen were marching out of tune and Errol was waving his arms far too much for his own good. And everyone else wasn't making any attempt to stay in line. They ran ahead and jumped the queue when it suited them. It was a right mess.

If James had his way it would be much different, and much better. For a start, **there would have to be a practice first. One hour after school before it got dark. James would have the steps worked out already on a sheet of** foolscap. They'd be lined up in groups of ten and everyone would wear a Boys' Brigade uniform with a shirt and tie, a blouse if they were a girl. And everyone would need a letter of permission from their parents or else they wouldn't be allowed to join the parade.

And it wouldn't be no 'Popeye the Sailor Man' neither. It would be something more special than that. There could only be one tune. The theme from *Animal Magic*. Just the thought of it brought tingles to James's toes. Everyone would laugh of course, they'd make fun and pull tongues at him. But they could do nothing about it because it was James's show now. And it would be in big bright lights over school windows.

THE JAMES SHOW.

James couldn't remember the first time he didn't like Miss Young but he knew he really hated her when she slapped him on the face because he told her he wasn't staying for detention and she couldn't make him, so there.

More spectacular than *The Gang Show*, more lights than *Live at the London Palladium*, and more sequins and pearls than Liberace. It would be on BBC1, BBC2 and ITV, and if there was another channel it would be on that too. TV sales would shoot through the roof because no one would want to watch it on their old set. And if there was anything important on like the FA Cup Final or Fanny Craddock cooking spotted dick then it would just have to wait.

Miss Young and Miss Ball had arrived at Greenheys at the same time. Two mini-skirts; Miss Ball with blonde hair and long legs, Miss Young with deep blue eyes and Anita Harris hair. And when they found out that Miss Young was to be their teacher for the whole year, James and his friends had bets on who would be the first one to throw bits of paper under her desk to get a good look up her skirt. **Because this was James's show, a Winterwonderland Spectacular in Glorious Technicolor, stupendous Cinemascope and Stereophonic Sound.**

There'd be a million violins, seventy-six trombones and a cor anglais like the one on *Blue Peter* last Monday. There would also be a steel band with a hundred pans playing all at once, exactly like Dad's favourite record, 'St Kitts at Night'. And not forgetting a dozen glockenspiels and tambourines, each with their own sheet of music because if they got it wrong then it was six hundred lines and detention after school.

'He thinks he's Mister High-and-Mighty because he's moving to Ashton-under-Lyne,' Miss Young had said to Miss Ball, that time in assembly when she thought no one could hear her.

'I'll give them six months then they'll be back here like the rest of them. You mark my words.'

And when Mr Boyle chose James and Carl for the school orchestra she said they could do what they flipping well liked as she'd given up caring.

'If Mr Boyle wants to waste his time then let him.'

And when they had the concert at the Free Trade Hall, the others said Miss Young was in a bad mood all day and shouted at everyone.

Every school would have the day off and there would be no arithmetic or spelling tests for a whole week so as there was no chance of anyone falling asleep during the

show, *THE JAMES SHOW*. And the grown-ups would have time off work as well, but only for a day because grown-ups would get in the way and spoil things. Mum would make tea and operate the spotlights, Dad could be a guard with a bright new blue uniform with silver buttons and a captain's hat. Felicia would be the head dancer in the march and Laura would just sit there and sulk because that would teach her to tell tales about James taking those Jammy Dodgers from the biscuit tin. And Rose would just be Rose and everyone would say, 'Oh, ain't she cute.'

No one was bothered about Miss Ball leaving Greenheys apart from Miss Young. She cried in Miss Ball's leaving assembly. Big red blotched eyes and runny mascara and sobbing without making a sound the way white people did. James didn't need to laugh, just seeing Miss Young clutching her hankie to her swollen nose was good enough. He knew she'd be the first one to break down, the first one to cry. No amount of slaps on the legs and being sent to Mr Boyle's office had made him cry, no way.

There would be only one place big enough. Princess Road, of course. It would have to be closed off for the week as well, and cobble-stoned from Aunty Vernice's house all the way down to Manchester Airport. And each house along Princess Road would have an enormous box full of party hats, whistles, streamers, hooters, and ticker tape to throw at the passing parade. And when they ran out of ticker tape then a man from the council would drive up and drop off a fresh box and he wouldn't ask for a penny neither.

A week before the parade there would a front page spread in all the newspapers, even the *Sun*, and on the telly there'd be so many adverts of the parade that there would have to be some on the BBC. The event of a lifetime, the spectacular of the century, superstars of superstars' extravaganza, with free popcorn as well. And everything would begin at 8 o'clock on the dot because that would give James enough time to finish his dinner and get changed. Fred Astaire and Ginger Rogers had promised to turn up as they were doing a show at the Palace Theatre, *Top Hat A Go-Go*. Blackpool Town Hall had promised to lend all their illuminated trams and lights as well as a million sixpences in case the meters ran out.

And what about snow, it had to snow even though the snow never stuck to the ground for long in Moss Side. That was easy to do. Just invite Bing Crosby to sing 'White Christmas'. Then there would be so much snow there would be enough left over for Boxing Day.

When Miss Young marked James wrong in spelling because he wrote brought instead of bought and she said don't argue with me you stupid boy, and James replied you're the one that's stupid not me, no one was the least bit surprised. After that she went so white and trembly she forgot to send him to Mr Boyle for the slipper. When James went back to his seat Carl couldn't stop laughing.

'You're dead you are, she's goner kill you.'

Luckily the bell went and everyone rushed out just in case and by the time they'd reached the playground the parade had already started.

Maybe James should invite the Queen, or Princess Anne. Or even the President of the United States, but he changed his mind as presidents had a bad habit of getting shot in the head – even their brothers. Forget the royalty and presidents, they could stay at home and watch on the

telly like everyone else. Because this was to be James's parade, *THE JAMES SHOW*, and it was for everyone from Moss Side to Timbuktu. And it would be a zillion times better than a bunch of school kids marching in the playground during morning playtime because anyone could do 'Popeye the Sailor Man', that was easy.

twelve

'I know what helps me sleep ... whoops, I forgot I've got company. No, James, don't ask.'

It was always like that, trying to fall asleep. You'd be in bed for ages with your eyes closed and nothing happening, then before you knew it, the sun was up and you felt the bed sheets and they were wet again. Just like that it was. One minute he was tossing and turning on the cold wooden floor. **The next he was on a country road by some bushes standing next to a pile of bottles of rum and there was a big guy with the cleanest teeth he'd ever seen and he was screaming blue murder at James. But as usual James couldn't understand a word he was saying.**

There were four of them, all of them grown-ups. It was just like at one of Aunty Vernice's parties. Grown-ups standing in the corner drinking rum and waiting for blood, steam coming out of their noses like Alsatian dogs on a cold day. It was just like one of Aunty Vernice's parties only it wasn't. It was back in the West Indies again and instead of trying to get food from the table in the front room where all the grown-ups were, James was selling rum to the four men and he'd accidentally dropped one of the bottles on this guy's foot.

James knew it was rum in the bottles and not water. It was just as Mum had said. When she was a little girl she used to sell rum by the road just like this. Rum which Papa used to brew in a large tank outside the house. A penny a bottle and watch out for the police, Aunty Vernice would say to Mum.

'And don't come back without no money or else.'

Money and the police were the last thing on James's mind at that moment. This guy looked like he was going to give James a good belting. His friends were laughing and jeering, egging him on.

'Go on,' they jeered, 'tell him they have no business moving house.'

The man smiled, showing a mouthful of gold teeth. 'You heard. When you get home you can tell Smallie and Coolie they got no business with them white people. You understand, boy?' Then he laughed and James could see his back teeth were also gold. At times like this James usually tried to look as frightened as possible, which wasn't too difficult. Usually this had the effect of causing the grown-ups to laugh at him and tell him to go about his business before they changed their mind; sometimes a sixpence was thrown in for good measure. And thank goodness it worked. That was too close for comfort. Next time, if there was a next time, he'd come with someone.

A grown-up, perhaps; a friend. Someone to protect him from large ladies with fingers missing and men with rum on their breaths.

thirteen

'Yes, I'm feeling fine, James. Kind of you to ask.'

Did they think he was stupid, or what? He knew what was going on. He knew what happened a few nights ago when someone banged on the front door and Dad went to see in case it was burglars. Then Dad called Mum into the entrance and told her to shut the living-room door. Even Felicia and Laura knew something was going on by now, especially when Mum said oh my God. Felicia tried to be all grown-up and told him and Laura to sit down and behave yourself or else.

All that was a few nights ago and now he had other things on his mind. The egg looked quite inviting there, in a cup with its top open showing hard egg-white and golden yolk all runny and yummy, begging to be dunked. And there by the side, bread soldiers all buttered and stood to attention. It wasn't his egg though, it wasn't his home neither. It was Miriam's, Mum's friend. Only Miriam wasn't there. Neither was Louise, Miriam's youngest and his girlfriend, Mum said, and Miriam said too. Only Heather, Miriam's big daughter, who was crying by the bed. Mum was there too, but she wasn't crying.

Did they think he was stupid, or what? He knew what went on all right. It was Mum who dragged him over in the first place. He wanted to play football with his friends, but Mum had insisted. But when he saw the egg – well, it was raining anyway. Mum and Miriam were best friends, even though Miriam had a few grey hairs and Mum had none. They were best friends only Miriam wasn't here and he knew why even without Felicia having to open her big fat gob. He knew about Louise too only he would never believe Felicia, not in a million years.

It was Heather's egg with soldiers, on the tray on the dressing table. It had to be, she was the only one in when Mum knocked on the front door and shouted *cooeee* through the letterbox. Heather was still crying and Mum was mumbling something really soppy and stupid so he reckoned no one wanted the egg any more. If it was Louise's egg she would have given him some. He'd have given her some if it was his. He would if he could but he couldn't because she wasn't there and never will be ever again, if Felicia wasn't lying. Besides, it wasn't his egg, it was Heather's and Heather was a grown-up now.

He liked her a lot, Louise. She was his best girlfriend. Only girlfriend, actually, but who was counting as Aunty Mary would say. He liked Heather too, but not as much. Heather was big and grown-up and had spots. There were no spots on Louise. He liked Louise a lot, even though she was nine and he was nine and a quarter. He liked the way he could run his fingers through her hair and it wouldn't get stuck. He liked her blue eyes so clear you could see right through her head. Not that he could look for long. She could always out-stare him. Not that she could right now as she wasn't there right now. He wished she was. She'd let him eat the egg, he was sure of that.

It was like any other bedroom really, with creased up clothes all over the place and the bed unmade but at least it didn't smell of pee. Heather sat by the dressing table, still in her nightie. Typical. If he'd been wearing his pyjamas at this time of the morning he'd be in dead trouble. He couldn't wait to grow up. When you were a grown-up you could leave your egg in its cup with its top open showing hard white and golden yolk all runny and yummy with bread soldiers all buttered and stood to attention just asking to be dunked and no one would say anything. Maybe he should ask if he could have some even though the answer would be No. It was always No with grown-ups, or shut up and behave yourself before you get what for.

Did they think he was stupid, or what? He knew what went on when the ambulance stopped outside Miriam's house the other night. Felicia and Laura tugging at the front-room curtains so they could get a better look, switching off the lights in case Mum and Dad saw them and sent them to bed. He knew it was an ambulance all right. He'd known for years now, ever since he was in the infants when Mrs Rowbottom showed one on a big white card. And now he was nine and a quarter and they were going to move to Ashton-under-Lyne at the end of the summer.

And at the time Felicia had said it was definite now, Louise would have to be put away in a home for good. James told her to shut her big fat mouth. Then Felicia said it didn't matter anyway because Louise's mother came from a home in the first place and when James called her a liar

Felicia said she did too because Mum said Aunty Mary had found Louise's mum on her doorstep one night when she was a little girl and James said Aunty Mary was never a little girl then Felicia said no Louise's mum stupid and James would have said I'll tell Mum on you for swearing only Felicia was giving a Chinese burn at the time so he thought better of it. And after she'd finished giving James a Chinese burn she went on about Aunty Mary not having any children of her own and there was no chance of that ever happening seeing as she wasn't married and James said Aunty Mary was married too, she was married to Arthur in the photograph on her mantelpiece. And Felicia just laughed at James and this time she forgot to give him a Chinese burn but went on laughing like she'd heard something really funny and then she said oh brother wait till you hear why Louise's mother did what she did oh boy oh brother and James said I don't want to know anyway which was a lie really and Felicia said oh yes you do but I'm not telling you anyway you're not big enough to know and again James said who wants to know anyway I sure don't and anyway Louise's mum has got a name you know she's called Miriam and Felicia said not any more she isn't and it didn't matter the least bit whatsoever anyway because Louise was going away to a home and that was that. And a couple of days later when everything went back to normal James told Mum about Felicia telling lies. He also asked why did Miriam do what she did anyway, Felicia wouldn't say nothing, it wasn't fair. Mum just sighed and shook her head saying that sister of yours doesn't know when to keep her big mouth shut at times.

Heather had stopped crying. Now she was just sitting there all red-eyed and blotchy and still in her night-dress.

And Mum stroked her hair just like Miriam should have done only Miriam wasn't there so she couldn't. If he was quick while no one was looking. If he was fast enough no one would know. And anyway, Mum always said it was a shame to let good food go to waste. A bread soldier was in his hand already. No need to rush, no need to panic. That egg wasn't going anywhere even though it was runny. He knew he should ask, but they would only say No.

'Have you anywhere to stay?'

'Me aunt's in Miles Platting. Louise is there already.'

'I thought you had no relatives? Mary said . . .'

'One of Mary's friends, you know what Mary was like, even when she's not around. We call all her friends Aunty, just a habit I suppose. They've got two kids already.'

'Someone to play with, that's good.'

'They were on the phone last night. God knows how they found out so soon. I mean, it's not as if Mary could, you know.'

'You never know with that woman.'

'Stranger things happen at sea, or something like that she was always saying.'

'She said a lot of things did Mary.'

'You can say that again. Still, Louise will be happy there you'll see. But tell me, Heather, what about you?'

'Oh, I'll be okay no worries.'

'Still working for Debenham's down Piccadilly?'

'I was offered promotion last week. Shop fitter. Ten bob a week extra.'

'Can't be bad.'

'Oh yeah, I thought so as well. Mum was chuffed at the time. Yeah, well, you can never tell what goes on inside.'

'You can't blame yourself girl. Suicide's no one's fault.'

'Never heard a thing, never heard a thing. I mean, if I hadn't made her a cup of Horlicks . . .'

And with that Heather started up with the crying again, only this time she shrugged her shoulders like she was laughing, and the shrugs got bigger and bigger despite Mum stroking her hair even faster, and the crying was much louder now, almost screaming so loud, he was sure he would have nightmares that night. He put back the bread soldier he had in his hand and tried to arrange them on the plate as they were before.

fourteen

'This is what happens when you eat cheese just before bedtime.'

James was up by the ceiling rose, a fancy plastering job like an upside down wedding cake with an electric cord through the middle. It was the cord that was stopping him from falling down to the floor to certain death. He would scream only his throat was sore and his head ached. He'd had the mumps and been in bed for over a week now. The first two days were great, no school or anything, and Mum brought the dinner up on a tray. But it wasn't fun no more and the fever had got worse and now he was up on the ceiling, praying.

'Our Father, who fart in heaven, hello be Thy name . . .'

Down below was his sleeping body, curled up and pyjamaed under Batman bed sheets. He could let go of course, but the last time he tried that it was only with quick reflexes that he'd grabbed the light bulb. And with a great deal of effort he'd climbed back up the electric cord. Now he was stuck, clinging on for dear life. Just like gym at school, with those big thick ropes that stretch down from the ceiling. James had no problem with those. He could stay on them all day, legs and arms wrapped round in a knot, looking at the others dancing around to the music from *Zorba the Greek*. But this wasn't the gym, and the electric cord wasn't as thick as the gym rope, and the screws to the ceiling rose were coming loose one by one and the cord was shredding, just like a Tom and Jerry cartoon.

'Thy will be done on earth as it is in heaven, I don't want to die, I don't want to die ... Aaaaah!!!' The next moment he was sitting up in bed, sweating like a pig. He stopped screaming when he saw Aunty Mary sitting at the end of the bed. She was in her night-gown and bedroom slippers, just like old times. She patted the sheets.

'Um, dry bed. Well done James. See, it's easy when you try.'

They sat there for a few minutes, remembering the old times of tea, cakes and grandfather clocks in the front room, and Joey the budgie chirping away in his cage.

'Just thought I'd pop over and see how you were. Came to see someone else to take them back with me but she'd left already. Good job for her sake as well, I was goner give her a piece of my mind I can tell you.' And when James asked what it was like in heaven, all she would say was, 'It's okay, I guess.'

James threw off the blankets and crossed his legs like he was in assembly.

'Do they have lemon fudgesicles up there?'

'Lemon fudgesicles?'

'They're like ice-lollies only much nicer, Dad says, and

Mum and our Felicia and Clarence Harriet Colleen...'

'Whoa, young man, steady on.'

'They're lovely. Everyone from back home says so. A man on a bike with a white trolley sells them.' James tried to impersonate his mum's voice.

'Your mother always had a sweet tooth.'

'Aunty Mary?'

'Yes, James?'

'If I can see you, does that mean I'm dead?'

Mary laughed to herself. 'From the mouths of babes.'

'Am I? Am I dead?'

'Do you want to be?'

James pondered the question. He knew better than to rush an answer. 'I don't think so. I'm too young, aren't I?'

'You're as young as you feel, young man, you're as young as you feel.'

'So do they have lemon fudgesicles up there, only I've got a sore throat with all that screaming.'

'Wait till you're better, then we'll see, okay?'

James didn't want to wait. 'Why can't I go now? Feel me head. See, I'm much better.'

'If it's there, it'll wait for you to get better.'

James fell back on to his pillow. All this talking was making him tired. Mary kissed his forehead.

'Come any time you like. You know how. I'll be there waiting, I promise. Besides, you can't fit a quart into a pint pot.'

James closed his eyes. It was good to see Aunty Mary again, even without the cakes and biscuits. She hadn't changed one bit. She was still as daft as a brush.

fifteen

'You can choose your children . . . no, that's not right either.'

Like Aunty Mary, Jake had lived in Cadogen Street for ever and ever, amen, only Jake was still alive and Aunty Mary was dead. He had a wooden leg from one of the wars – James didn't know which one because Jake never said – but that didn't stop him from having a pile of records in his front room. He also worked for the council offices until they gave him a gold clock and told him not to come back.

'Maria Callas, *Diva*,' sighed Jake as he played James an old scratchy record of a lady singing high notes all the time. You could tell his children had grown up. A cupboard with all those records lined up like that wouldn't have lasted a minute in James's house.

James wasn't old enough to have seen Jake's children.

'They're as big as your mum and dad,' Jake said but that was all. He didn't talk about them much which was unusual for Jake. Records, old films, football teams, Mae West, Ruby Murray, Thomas Beecham's powders. As Aunty Mary would say, he could talk about anything under the sun, which seemed a pretty good way to get hot under the collar, another of Aunty Mary's sayings – James didn't understand that one neither. Now Mavis, Jake's wife, she never talked about anything at all, not when James was there. She'd be in the kitchen, or in the backyard pruning the privets, or anything else that urgently needed doing right this minute.

Another of Jake's favourite topics was his grandchildren, he was always talking about his grandchildren.

'Our Simon built a remote-controlled car,' Jake would say. Or 'Nigel came top in maths with 100% again.'

It was like watching *Panorama* or *World in Action* when Jake went on about his grandchildren. By the time he'd finished James would be ready for bed. But thankfully Jake talked about other things most of the time.

'Cigarettes, cans of Bovril, chocolate, you had to have tokens or else you couldn't get any of them during the *war*. And the streets weren't allowed to have no lights in case of the bombs. And the whole of Fernleaf Street was blown up at five to nine, the kids couldn't go to school for ages because of all the dust everywhere.'

James would've liked to have been in Cadogen Street during the war, it sounded like fun.

There wasn't anything Jake didn't know. How many furlongs in a mile, the bus fare to Piccadilly during the rush hour, how many people died when the bomb blew up Fernleaf Street, how to spell Hugo Montenegr. He even had the *Glenn Miller Story* on record, the film on the telly last Sunday. The whole family had watched it, even Dad, and James enjoyed it so much he made up a new game with Felicia and Laura where James played the trumpet, Felicia played the trombone and Laura played the drums even though she wanted to play the violin. James had insisted and Felicia agreed.

'They didn't play violins in the war.'

Jake agreed when James told him the next day and when Jake stood on a stool so he could reach the top shelf and when he brought down an almost brand new record with a picture of James Stewart in a major's uniform holding a trombone, James was so happy he could hear violins.

'Little Brown Jug', 'Moonlight Serenade', 'American Patrol'. It even had the dates when they were recorded. 'String of Pearls', 9 April 1939, 'Little Brown Jug', 10 June 1941. And later on when Jake gave the record to James to give to his mum as he had so many records one less wouldn't make any difference whatsoever, Mum said she was born in 1941.

'You're as old as "Little Brown Jug",' said James and they played the record just to make sure.

Jake said he bought the record in town, a record shop in Deansgate.

'Two and six it were. John was studying for his school certificate at the time,' said Jake, then he looked down at the carpet like he'd just remembered he wasn't supposed to speak about his own children under no circumstances whatsoever.

'American Patrol', 1941. 'Chattanooga Choo Choo', 1942.

'No streetlights were allowed after six and everyone had black curtains.'

Mum would love that, thought James, she hated washing curtains.

'A tram ride from Great Western Street to Central Station cost a ha'penny.'

'My Prayer', 30 June 1943.

James had seen Jake's wooden leg just the once, it was pink with holes in. And when he tapped it, it made a clang.

'Can I have one?' asked James at the time, and Jake just laughed, patted his head and said nothing.

'Perfidia', 20 August 1942. This one wasn't on the film but James liked it just the same and later or when James asked Dad what he did in the war all Dad would say was that he remembered some boys running down the lane shouting *Hitler coming* and everyone ran inside and locked all the doors and for weeks there was no rice, and what rice there was had sawdust and beetles in it.

'Apart from that, I don't remember a thing. I thought your mother said it was time for bed.'

The film was right, Glenn Miller did die in the war.

'A lot of good folk died in the war,' said Jake as he took his hankie out and blew his nose.

'Glenn Miller was in England with his band playing to cheer everyone up. We needed cheering up in the war,' said Jake as he rubbed his wooden leg like it was itchy. James couldn't understand why. With all the blitsing, blackouts, rationing and Fernleaf Street blowing up in the middle of the night, that was enough fun for anyone as far as James was concerned.

Simon and Nigel were due to visit that very afternoon so Mavis hadn't needed an excuse to go into the kitchen. There was baking to be done. Cakes, pies, corned-beef sandwiches, and lashings of ginger beer.

'They love me to read Enid Blyton. You've heard of Enid Blyton, haven't you?' said Jake. And James said of course he had. Enid Blyton was Felicia's favourite too. She would read them to James and Laura. *Mallory Towers*, *Claudine at*

St Clare's, anything at St Clare's. Anything with jolly hockey sticks, stink bombs, school uniforms, French mistresses and midnight feasts. James especially liked the midnight feasts. So when Jake said that he would read Enid Blyton to his grandchildren and Mavis would bake them cakes and pies and lashings of ginger beer and pretend it was a midnight feast even though they were only allowed to visit in the afternoon. James wished he could stay and join in perhaps, you know, to see what it was like. But he knew better than to ask. Mum was always saying to James that it was okay to visit the neighbours but not to over-stay your welcome – you never know with those white people. James didn't know exactly what she meant by that. But what he did know was that even though Jake was a very very nice man, it was not like Aunty Mary's where you could stay all day and there'd be tea and biscuits to pass the time. With Jake you had to let him do all the talking and as long as you sat quiet on the mat with your feet crossed then you were okay. And when he mentioned either Simon or Nigel you had to smile and look happy. And when he gave you an old comic or a old Dinky car that had been in the family for years, then you had to look really surprised like you'd won the pools or something when really that was the only reason why you were there in the first place. So when Jake showed James the present he'd bought for Simon, a Scalectrix set exactly like the one off the telly, that was easy enough.

'Wow wee, that's really great. They'll love that, I know I would.'

And they did like them and on each time the brand new Ford Cortina only stayed for five minutes which was more than enough time for Simon and Nigel to collect their presents and say hello to their grandma.

And later on that day James heard Jake talking with Mum.

'Families,' said Jake. 'You can choose your friends but you can't choose your family,' he said.

'You can say that again. Look at me aunty. I said she can come any time she likes, bring Uncle Luke, bring the lot of them, it's okay I said – till I'm blue in the face. It's not wrong is it, wanting to move? I mean, we can't stay here all our lives. You have to move on. It's only natural, isn't it?'

'You can move on too much sometimes. Look at our John. You'd think he was ashamed of us or something. Whenever he visits with the kids he never stops. He just drops them off and that's it. Won't even stop for tea, him and that wife of his. Talk about fur coat and no knickers.'

'Is that what they're like when they grow up?' said Mum without looking up from the sewing machine.

And at the time Jake just nodded his head like one of those toy dogs you see at the back of cars.

'Not all of them, thank goodness, only your own,' said Jake.

' "Pennsylvania six five thousand". That's my favourite,' said James.

' "String of Pearls" is mine,' said Jake. 'You wouldn't believe it but it was the Number One of our day.'

'Wow,' said James, 'was it really?'

'We didn't have *Top of the Pops* in those days.'

'Can I have a feel of the record cover please?' Jake passed James the record sleeve. James felt the almost brand new shiny edge along his fingers. He could imagine what it was like when Jake first brought the record home to his wife and child, they must've been over the moon. Just like James had been when he saw the *Glenn Miller Story* last Sunday.

He was so excited he couldn't eat his dinner. James had never seen a film with so much good music. All the tunes made you want to get up on your feet and dance the boogie woogie, which Felicia did because she could do any dance she liked could Felicia. And when Glenn Miller went missing over the English Channel at the end of the film James wasn't too sad because he might still be there after all these years, floating in a bath or something, or even an old settee, writing more songs for when he's rescued. And they'd be Number One too, even on *Top of the Pops*.

'In the Mood'. The third of September, nineteen hundred and forty-three, the last tune recorded before he departed on the ill-fated English tour.

'What does ill-fated mean?' asked James. Jake didn't answer, instead he took the record from the turntable and put it back in the sleeve. And as if he knew what James had been thinking all afternoon he presented James with the record like he was giving out a school certificate.

'It would only gather dust up there anyway.'

'At Last', 20 August 1941.

sixteen

'A different ending? I should hope so. I've got better things to do than watch repeats.'

Once again, Cadogen Street had a strange look to it as day turned to dark. Only this time there was nothing but a full moon and a nightful of stars. Not that Aunty Mary had noticed any of this. All she could see were the boarded up houses with 'X' painted over the front doors. She'd come as promised and was sitting in the middle of the road on an old deck-chair, knitting busily like she'd never been away.

'Tut tut tut. What a mess. And what's that, may I ask?' she said, pointing to a broken down lamp-post that had fallen into the middle of the street.

'Some men in a car ran into it. They were going dead fast,' said James.

'Arthur would've made a phone call to the council

by now and no mistake.' But James was too pleased to see her to worry about such things.

'Thanks for coming, Aunty Mary.'

'My pleasure, young man. We'll look for lemon fudgesicles another time, eh?'

'You believe me, don't you?'

'Of course I do, James.'

He needn't have worried whether Aunty Mary believed him or not, because at that very moment a drum roll began and the moon shone a spotlight on James like he was the star of the *Saturday Show*. Mary put her knitting down.

'Is that it?'

'No,' said James, 'there's more.'

And sure enough, the spotlight swung over to Number 22 followed by shouting and screaming and the slamming of doors.

'Oh dear. I see what you mean.'

'See, I told you. You have to help now.'

Cadogen Street had a strange look to it as day turned to dark. The monsters and dragons in the walls had fallen asleep by then, and the moonlit river of silver trout had finally come to rest. Aunty Mary had gone by now but not before she'd promised to do something.

'God knows what or let the devil take the high road,' she'd said before disappearing when no one was looking. Now James was left outside, and he wasn't going anywhere until the sobbing stopped; once again.

seventeen

'Like I said before. Too much telly.'

It could've been straight out of *The Flaxton Boys*, a telly programme where two boys run down a hill in the Yorkshire Moors, accompanied by an orchestra of strings. Only this wasn't the Yorkshire Moors, or even ITV. It was Brimstone Hill in St Kitts, the same Brimstone Hill where the British had kicked out the French and built a fort to stop them from coming back. The same Brimstone Hill where James had found a pair of binoculars and was now looking down on to the big white house in the valley below.

These were the best binoculars James had ever seen. They had rubber all over and if you dropped them on the floor they would bounce right back into your hands. They also had knobs you twiddled to get a better view.

The house was exactly as Mum described. A big white house with a porch, veranda and four large rooms not including the kitchen and bathroom. 'Like the house on *Bonanza*,' Mum said. She said it took ages to clean them big houses but you were grateful for the work because at least it was all the year round, not like cutting sugar-cane or picking cotton which you could only do in the crop season. 'If you were caught stealing Mr Orson would sack you on the spot and then you'd have to leave the village and find somewhere else to live.'

There was a bush by the side which was full of fruits that looked like lemons. But when he looked closer they were more like furry grapes. And when he squeezed one between his fingers a big stone plopped out, just like a cherry. James licked his fingers. Umm strawberry. Things were funny like that in the West Indies. Rain that chased you down the road, centipedes as big as your arm, hurricanes that blew houses all the way from Basseterre to Dieppe Bay, stars that fell out of the sky. So when James heard screaming noises from the house down below, he wasn't the least bit surprised.

Mr Orson was the white man who owned all the cane fields and the big white house. He always wore a freshly starched white shirt every day, Mum said. So when James saw a man with a face as white and stiff as his shirt collar gripping a struggling calf with one hand whilst holding a shaving knife in the other, James didn't need to ask who it was. The man was trying to put the calf into an old bath-tub full of water. But the calf probably guessed it wasn't to have a bath the way it kicked and bleated. And sure enough, with a swish of the knife the calf's head dropped down into the tub with a plop.

Mrs Orson was even paler than Mr Orson, Mum said, because she stayed indoors all day playing the piano and baking cakes. And at church every Sunday Mr and Mrs Orson would sit far away from everyone else because they were the only ones with a hymn book.

James wasn't surprised when the calf's head dropped off because Mum had said it would. What he didn't expect was all that blood. It was everywhere, spewing from its neck like a water fight. Squirt, squirt, squirt all over the place until the only thing that wasn't red was Mr Orson's shirt. Mum said he did that to all the male calves from his prize-winning cow so that no one else could have one. With all that blood it could have been a late-night horror film with Boris Karloff and Christopher Lee, so scary that even the grown-ups would wake up in a wet bed screaming Mummy.

eighteen

'With friends like that who needs enemies.'

It was a Wednesday like any other Wednesday. Games after morning assembly. Games in the infants meant running around in your vest and pants to the 'Dance of the Trolls' from *Peer Gynt* or the music from *Zorba the Greek*. Everyone would jump about with their arms in the air pretending the trolls were chasing them under the bridge and when it came to the exciting part near the end all the girls would scream and all the boys would laugh, apart from James because he wanted to scream like the girls but he couldn't so he had to laugh instead. But that was in the infants. Now James was in the juniors and games in the juniors meant football in the winter and cricket in the summer. Going to the park and playing against the older boys in the big class with a real cricket ball that you could hardly lift never mind bowl. And when it was your turn to bat you made sure you were bowled out first ball just in case you got hit by the next ball, especially if Errol was bowling. And by the time the game was finished it was time for lunch and Mr Jones would let everyone run back to school as part of the exercise – in fact he insisted or else. And if the game finished early they could go to the front of the dinner queue before anyone else.

But not today. James was the last one to bat and they only needed ten more runs to win and after the ball hits your bat a couple of times you get used to the shock. The others didn't like that one bit even though they were on his team. They didn't like the idea of missing the start of the dinner queue and they let James know exactly what they thought.

'Wait till we get back,' screamed Carl. 'I'm goner kick your head in,' which everyone knew was stupid because the last time Carl tried something like that James gave him a bloody nose.

The only one not screaming at James was Mr Jones. He just smiled.

'What a shame you're leaving. You'd be on the school team otherwise.'

And when the next ball hit the middle of the bat and the ball went to the left past the fielders with James and Roy taking a run, James decided he might just stick around for a bit longer. Besides, it had been the last ball of the over and he felt good enough to face another six balls. The groans from his so-called team-mates were loud enough for the dinner ladies to hear back at the school which was at least a five minute sprint even if you took a short cut down the alley off Monton Street. One of the big boys was bowling now, Carlton or something, you didn't speak to the big boys unless they were beating you up. So when the ball whizzed past his ears and went straight past the wicketkeeper and to the boundary without bouncing, James wasn't the least bit surprised.

Now it was Gary's turn to give James encouragement. 'Run the next one, even if you don't hit it,' he said. But James took no notice as he'd seen Gary whispering to Roy just before the previous ball, and he still hadn't forgotten the time Gary told everyone that people who wet their beds weren't allowed to live in a brand new house anywhere, never mind Ashton-under-Lyne. So when James pretended to run the next ball and Roy looked away like he'd seen something else, again James wasn't the least bit surprised.

The next two balls were okay, one just missed the left-hand bails to cries of *ooh you jammy bugger* from the fielders, and the next ball hit James's bat just before he dropped it to the ground with the ball going in the air and falling between the running fielders on the boundary. Which was just as well as it had been the last ball of the over. Errol joined in now, only he was more honest than Gary or Carl. He just ran up to James and clenched his fists to his face. 'Get out the next ball or I'll kick your fucking teeth in.' And if Mr Jones hadn't come running up to them to separate them, he would've done too.

After that, James decided he wasn't taking no chances, so he walked up to Roy at the other end of the crease. 'You run me out and I won't help you with arithmetic no more.'

Mr Jones ran up to James and patted him on the back. 'You're doing well, son, keep it up. Only three more runs to win.'

If Mr Jones was trying to make James feel nervous then he succeeded. And when the next ball just missed his head as he fell to the floor again, his heartbeat went up so loud even the worms could hear.

Count to ten backwards, ten, nine, eight. Count to one

hundred backwards, to a thousand? Concentrate, must concentrate. It's only a ball, I mean, what harm can it do, eh? It's only a rock hard solid ball coming at me at a million miles an hour, that's all, that's all. Don't shake, don't shake, can't help it can't help.

'*Oh no.*'

The ball edged off James's bat and went into the wicket-keeper's hand, but not before it had bounced twice.

Stop shaking, stop shaking, I'm goner die. Help me God, me heart's beating so fast it's goner burst like a balloon and all me blood will spill out on to the floor. I'm goner die, Mr Boyle Mr Boyle Mr Boyle? Yes Mr Boyle choir practice, it can't be worse than choir practice, nothing can be worse than choir practice, me heart I can feel it going slower. Mr Boyle Mr Boyle nothing's worse than Mr Boyle when you sing a note wrong. Mr Boyle Mr Boyle screaming blue murder, this is easy this is *so* easy.

So when the next ball hit the middle of the bat and went past Mr Jones's diving fingers and everyone else's before smacking into the green fence that was the boundary, James wasn't the least bit surprised. But he was surprised when the whole of his team began to cheer from the sidelines, and when they ran up to him they threw him in the air like he was a hero. Which he was when somebody eventually told him that he'd just scored the winning run.

Mr Jones was pleased even though his team had lost. 'Well done, James, especially under pressure like that.'

James thanked him even though if he'd realised only one run was needed he would've wet his pants, or even worse. Thankfully Errol had forgotten about his threat to James to bash him in, and was now carrying him on his shoulder back to the park gates, whilst Gary and Carl followed behind. They'd said nothing even when the others had been cheering so James knew something was up. And sure enough when they got back to school and James returned from the toilet after collecting his dinner of meat pie and chips, he found in his place a different plate with a smaller piece of pie and a lot less chips. Someone had either swopped dinners or eaten some of his. Gary and Carl just smiled and said nothing. James knew it was Carl's idea, Gary wouldn't have the nerve. But he didn't say anything during dinner and for the rest of the day, even during the afternoon playtime. And when James went home that evening and asked Mum if he could have lunch at home and she said yes, he was so pleased that the next day the first thing he did was to punch Carl in the face.

nineteen

'I don't care what you say. We *have* been here before.'

James turned to Aunty Mary. 'You said you'd do something. You promised.'

Aunty Mary patted the bowl of fruit on her head, as it kept on tilting like the Leaning Tower of Pisa. Maybe it wasn't such a good idea to come as Carmen Miranda after all. 'In a minute, young man. Only I'm not sure if I've enough hat pins. Too many and there's fruit juice all over the place.'

The dancing was the same as before, with Mr Green still on the night shift. They even did a hop, skip, turn-around to prove the point, again. James tugged at Aunty Mary's sleeves.

'Hey, steady on. Next time I'll use plastic. What do you think, James?'

'She'll be here any moment, hurry.'

'What's your favourite colour?' And when James told her to stop messing about she just went on and on. 'I never told you, I never married you know. Arthur was just a name I made up. The photo on the mantelpiece, well I'm glad you mentioned that. December 1948, the annual jumble sale at Christ Church, tuppence ha'penny.'

'Oh Aunty Mary, please. Once she's gone then that'll be it. Then it's too late.'

'Red, green, aquamarine? There was always someone close though, someone special, long before your lot came over,' and she winked at James like he knew who that special someone was.

'You promised, you said you'd do something. I hate you.'

'Couldn't say anything of course, with him being married and working for the council and all,' and again she winked at James before saying, 'It's blue isn't it?'

'I really mean it, I hate you.'

'Don't be daft. You're not old enough. So which is it?'

'Blue.'

'See, I told you.' And she grabbed a banana before it fell to the floor.

'There, now – look over there,' and she pointed to Number 22, the Jacksons' house. Suddenly the music stopped and everyone had stopped dancing and gone indoors. And just as suddenly it was night time with the street lights on and the curtains closed. 'Good job you said blue. If you'd said red, oh boy.' She shoved James in the back. 'On your way, young man. I've done my bit, now it's your turn.'

'I still hate you, Aunty Mary.'

'Of course you do. Now hurry along before the meter runs out.'

twenty

'This one's my favourite, Aunty Mary.'

'James, you'll be sick,' said Mum, but that didn't stop him from biting into the juicy meat slab with onions and tomato ketchup covered by two halves of a muffin. Hamburgers, James's favourite. It had to be Blackpool too, or else it wasn't the same. The day trip to the seaside by coach without Dad. Dads never went to the seaside. Dads never had holidays, they weren't allowed. They went to work instead, usually before the sun was up, and they'd return after the sun went down again. For fun they watched racing and Sunday league cricket. On the telly of course, or else it wasn't fun. And at Christmas all the dads would come round to eat a big pot of pigs' feet and drink rum and dunk the bread and talk about the good old days back home where they would bang steel pans and play masquerade in the carnival. They would go back to work the day after Boxing Day because dads weren't allowed any more fun. That was why dads never went to the seaside.

'Serves you right, you pig, don't say I didn't warn you,'

said Mum as she wiped his mouth with a hankie. As well as the hamburger, James had also eaten a packed lunch of salami sandwiches, crisps, doughnuts and candyfloss and had brought most of it up behind the stall next to the dodgems. Felicia and Laura were killing themselves laughing and James would hit them only Mum hadn't finished wiping his mouth. 'You're no better than Rose,' said Mum. She was right too. Even though Rose was the cutest toddler there ever was, she was always being sick, especially over the carpet or on Uncle Mason's lap. James reckoned Rose was sick even before she was born because Mum was never out of the toilet when Rose was in her stomach. A lot of things were different just before Rose was born. Dad did the cooking because Mum was too big to come downstairs. A nurse came every day for three weeks and made her own tea. Apart from that, things were normal until Wednesday, 9 August 1967, when Clarence, Harriet, Deniece, Benjamin and Colleen came for a party downstairs while the nurse stayed upstairs with Mum. And even though they were cousins Clarence, Harriet, Deniece, Benjamin and Colleen were big enough to be with the other grown-ups at the food table at Aunty Vernice's Saturday night parties. Clarence and Harriet were so big they didn't even go to school. Clarence was a car mechanic and wore oily overalls and screwdrivers in the back pocket and Harriet was a nurse in the building just across Great Western Street and Greenheys School. And at playtime, James would wave to her and if she remembered she would wave back and James would say to the others see I told you she was me cousin. Deniece, Benjamin and Colleen weren't big enough to be a nurse or a car mechanic but they were big enough to go to that really big school on a corner by the side of Princess

Road. It was so big they didn't even have to take an 11-plus like in Felicia's school.

Clarence made up a game without a name but it was really fun all the same. The game was to guess the film star from the initials, the clues being the films they'd starred in. When it was James's turn everyone fell about in stitches when he said DW, because everyone knew James's favourite programme was *Doctor Who*, and they didn't stop laughing until Dad ran downstairs at eight o'clock in the evening.

James had wanted a brother. The other one, Franklin, had died when the hole in his heart leaked the blood out. But when he saw the little pink bundle wrapped up in Mum's arms, he was glad she was a girl. Mum looked flushed like she'd done a really big poo. Afterwards, Felicia and Deniece made some corned beef sandwiches and a pot of tea and Clarence taught everyone how to play Gin Rummy. The next morning the bundle of sleeping pink flesh was now a lovely lump of Afro hair and chubby cheeks.

'Charlie Drake', everyone agreed, and she was stuck with the name, until the vicar changed it to Rose Judith over the church sink. She was still looking like Charlie Drake when they had their pictures taken at Brown's Photographer's on Princess Road. James wouldn't stop fidgeting and hitting Laura. It was all right for her, she didn't have to wear a suit with short pants, a polyester shirt and an elastic tie. Dad gave James one of those looks that meant if you don't keep your backside still you won't have a backside to sit on when I've done with you. So by the time of the family photo everyone was so well behaved the cameraman didn't need the rubber duck.

It was the fastest James had seen Rose crawl, that Sunday

afternoon when Aunty Vernice stopped her visits with ice-cream. James was playing ball against the entrance wall. Thump, thump, thump, just inside the flowered patterns. If Dad caught him, he'd be in dead trouble. It was the last thump that did it. James put a bit more effort in, like you do when you're bowling to Gary Sobers. Thump. He didn't know she was at the bottom of the stairs. Thump. It was only the sight of a nappied little bum flashing past that gave it away. She zoomed right into the living room and wouldn't have stopped if Felicia hadn't grabbed her by the safety pins. That was why Mum and Dad waited until Rose could walk before going on the holiday of a lifetime back to the West Indies. It was a good job too. When they returned, Mum went straight to bed to be ill and she didn't get up until ages afterwards.

While Mum and Dad were on their holiday of a lifetime, Rose had been left with Mrs Powell whilst the others stayed at Princess Road with Aunty Vernice, Uncle Luke, Clarence, Harriet, Deniece, Benjamin and Colleen. Always a houseful of grown-ups, staying up late even on a schoolday, sneaking into the girls' bedroom while they got dressed, pretending he didn't know what a girdle was. Cod liver oil on the dressing table; little yellow bubbles in a plastic bag which you swallowed like an aspirin. No need for Felicia to grab your nose and stamp your toes. The highlight of the stay was watching the late-night horror movie *City of the Dead* with Christopher Lee. It was on so late, the lights were left off to save electricity, Clarence said. James huddled between Benjamin and Harriet, thinking he'd be safe from the ghosts and vampires, but little did he know. And when the man in the mask and a long black cloak stabbed the woman on the table through the heart, James would have fallen off the settee if Benjamin hadn't grabbed his legs. Felicia said she wasn't scared and James agreed because she'd had her head under the cushion all night.

Yes, as far as James was concerned, Mum and Dad could stay in the West Indies forever and ever amen. James had nightmares for a long time after that, even when Mum and Dad came back with a bagful of mangoes and rotting cassava and Mum went to bed sick.

Hot buttered toast for breakfast. Uncle Luke had a big mug of a punch made from condensed milk, eggs, rum, stout and strawberry syrup before going to work at the Dunlop factory that smelt of burnt tyres. Saturday afternoons and a kitchen full of flour, salt and red snappers spitting in a pan. Aunty Vernice said it was her duty to fry fish for everyone in Moss Side, even though her kitchen was only big enough for a cooker and a sink. Mum said she would fry fish for Raymond herself and Aunty said no one could fry fish like me so Mum said there's nothing you can do about it he's my husband, before filling Rose's bottle with warm blackcurrant.

The ghost train at Blackpool was the most dangerous ghost train in the world, Felicia said. It was so scary a man screamed so hard he choked to death on his dentures. At least the penny arcades were safe; slot machines with arms that went *kerchunk* with pictures of oranges, lemons and stars. If you got three of a kind you got the pennies back with a few more besides. Mum's favourite was the horse races. Six of them – red, blue, green, brown, yellow and white. A red bet won a penny, up to twelve pence for a white win. Mum always bet white. 'I know what I'm doing,' she said, even though it only won once.

She also said she knew what she was doing when she got

out of her sick bed and told everyone she was going to college to learn dressmaking. 'You get more money making clothes than bras.' She also said something about looking for a new house, but no one understood her at the time. So after two years of walking three miles to Hollins College every Monday and Tuesday, Mum got a City and Guilds on a sheet of paper and a kiss from Dad. James and Laura jumped up and down on the settee. Felicia was doing her homework upstairs and Rose didn't know any better, so she cried instead. Aunty Vernice, Uncle Luke, Clarence, Harriet, Deniece, Benjamin and Colleen didn't say anything because they didn't know anything about it until Mum gave Aunty Vernice the phone number of their new house in Ashton-under-Lyne. Mum insisted the telephone was there already.

'What do you want a phone for?' said Aunty Vernice. 'Will you be too busy to come back and visit?'

twenty-one

'Ships sinking, okay. Lemon fudgesicles, maybe. But Kenneth More?'

It was like waiting for a bus, the 53 on Great Western Street outside Greenheys School. The 53 used to be a trolley bus when all the buses were trolley buses. A crisscross of wires crossed the skies which it followed with two long rods sticking out of its roof. James was just old enough to remember them. That and the smog so thick you bumped into lamp-posts, smog so thick the rods on the trolley buses would fall off and you had to wait until a man with a big stick put them back on again. Sometimes the man with the big stick wouldn't turn up so you had to walk home and you'd be so tired you'd want to go to bed but you couldn't because you had to cook salt fish and cornmeal for Aunty Vernice and Uncle Luke because you would always be grateful to them for paying your passage over to England because it was hard for a young mother to raise a baby all by herself, Mum said. But this wasn't Great Western Street, or Moss Side or even the number 53. It was the port in Basseterre, the capital of St Kitts, 'Town' as people from back home called it. James and Aunty Mary were at the end of the queue waiting for the ferry to take them over to Nevis. It wasn't James's idea to board the *Christina*. He'd told Aunty Mary that it had sunk on the telly but she would have none of it.

'You want a lemon fudgesicle or what?' said Aunty Mary.

'Why can't we stay here for them?' said James.

'Because we can't so don't argue.'

James resisted Mary's pushing. 'I don't want to die, not yet anyway.'

Mary patted his head. 'You won't die, I promise. Besides, nothing is ever certain, James, but death and taxes.' And before James could ask her what the hell she meant the whistle blew for everyone to board.

'I've never been to a Caribbean carnival before, might be fun,' said Aunty Mary.

A Night to Remember, the film of the sinking of the *Titanic*, with Kenneth More. At the end of the film he ended up in a lifeboat with some women and children. Meanwhile the ship was sinking with a lot of people still on board, and all this while the brass band played tiddly om pom pom. It had been like that aboard the *Christina*, only there were a lot more coloured people. It was as if they'd seen the film the night before and knew all the parts by heart. And instead of a brass band there was a steel band. But apart from that it could have been straight off the film.

The Captain boomed instructions through his megaphone: 'Everyone with blue tickets go into the lifeboats, anyone with red tickets must wait on board for further instructions.'

James raised his right hand. 'Please sir, I haven't got ...' a slap from Aunty Mary stopped him in mid-flow.

'Silence is a girl's best friend, James.'

'But I'm a boy,' said James, still rubbing his head.

'Well someone has to be,' said Aunty Mary as she opened up her purse revealing two blue tickets. 'If anyone asks, you're with me.'

'Thank you, my good man,' said Aunty Mary to the half-caste man collecting the tickets by the lifeboat. He didn't look pleased one bit, especially with James. He stared at the ticket and then at James and back to the ticket as if somebody was telling fibs. Aunty Mary whispered to James, 'Is he a cousin of yours?'

James was too scared to answer, the half-caste man was giving him really evil looks by now. Maybe it had something to do with James being the only coloured person on board the lifeboat. No, it had to be his T-shirt. It had tomato ketchup stains from last night's fish and chips.

The lifeboat had rowed far from the boat by now, the shouting and screaming were now only a blur. A dim and distant memory about a mile down the sea.

'Fathoms,' said Aunty Mary. 'You don't have miles at sea.'

'Still,' said James, determined to have the last word for once, 'it's a long way away.'

'To Tipperary,' said Aunty Mary.

'Tipperary?'

'Yes, Tipperary.'

'Is it anywhere near Abergavenny?'

'Abergavenny?'

'Yes, Abergavenny,' said James. 'It's a song, Number One.'

Now it was Aunty Mary's turn to look confused. 'Number One?'

James decided this was a good moment to teach her the words of the song.

Mary sighed. Unfortunately she knew the words. There was no way out, this being a lifeboat and the others being such miserable buggers. So she sang along, in descant, of course, ♪bum bum bum♪ and the next bit was where the brass band really did play tiddly om pom pom, but there wasn't enough room on the lifeboat so James and Aunty Mary pretended to play kazoos instead.

The others just sat there, they were determined not to enjoy themselves.

'Miserable buggers.'

'Maybe they don't have pop charts over here,' said James.

'Pop charts?' asked Aunty Mary.

'The charts, the Hip Parade.'

'You've lost me even more now.'

'Jimmy Savile, Tony Blackburn, you know, *Top of the Pops*.'

'How many times have I told you not to watch that rubbish. It'll shrink your brains, mark my words young man,' said Mary. She had a look on her like she was trying hard to be vexed but she completely spoilt the effect by taking out of her bag a bundle wrapped up in a towel and unwrapping it.

'Buttered scones?'

And James would've had one too only he was distracted by something in the water. It was a fat black woman bobbing up and down in the water like she couldn't make her mind up whether to sink or swim.

'Hello lady,' said James.

The woman didn't answer and continued to tread water.

James tried again. 'I know you, don't you live on our street?'

Mary turned round. 'What on earth are you doing?'

'It's okay, I know her I think.' And with that he proceeded to stick his foot into the water.

'James, get back in the boat this minute, you'll catch your death.'

'It's all right, I know what I'm doing, I've done this before.'

Mary had seen the woman in the water by now. 'Oh James, be careful. I don't want your mother telling me off for giving you pneumonia.'

'It's all right. Hold me arms to stop me falling in.'

Suddenly the woman in the water shouted, 'Go away, leave me alone, I'll find me own way, thank you.'

'Charming,' said Aunty Mary. 'There's no pleasing some people.'

James tried again. 'Come on lady, there's more than enough room.' He looked at the others for reassurance but none came. Instead they looked away like he had just farted. 'See, there's more than enough room, isn't there Aunty Mary?'

'Take no notice of the others, James,' said Mary, then

she turned round to face them. 'Good manners won't hurt a flea,' she said before turning to the woman in the water. 'Come on out, love. Don't worry, they won't bite.'

The woman tried to say something but the splashing waves got in the way. Mary put her hand to her ear. 'Sorry dear, I didn't quite catch you.'

The woman cleared her throat. 'I said I've got a red ticket.'

Mary and James looked at each other and nodded. 'Come on love, there's lots of room, look.' Mary patted the space next to her. 'James can sit on my knee.'

James would've said like hell I will but he wasn't allowed to swear so he gave Aunty Mary a dirty look instead.

The woman in the water shook her head. 'I'm not allowed, the Captain said.'

'How about some scones? You people like scones, don't you?' said Aunty Mary, turning to James for reassurance.

'Maybe she doesn't like butter.'

'Doesn't like butter? Don't be silly James, everyone likes butter.'

'Me Dad don't.'

Mary looked at James like he'd just farted again. 'How can anyone not like butter?'

'And me Uncle Luke and Errol's dad and Mrs Best across the road, they don't like butter neither.'

'Enid too? Oh dear oh dear . . .'

'Me dad likes his bread in big pieces too,' said James.

'In big pieces?'

'Like this.' And James put his hands out like he'd caught a big fish.

'My goodness,' Mary sighed. 'And no butter?'

'No butter,' said James.

Mary looked up at the skies. 'I hadn't noticed how blue the skies are over here, a deep blue, almost purple like.'

'Are you okay, Aunty Mary?'

'I've a good mind to let her stay in the water . . . oh what the hell.' And she shouted to the woman and stretched out her hands. 'If anyone asks, you don't live round here, okay? Say you're visiting a sick friend and you have absolutely no intention whatsoever of moving in next door.'

twenty-two

'They have telly at school? What is the world coming to?'

There had been nothing else on the telly for ages, not even cartoons. Just fuzzy black and white pictures of men in white suits, hopping about on a beach of grey sand and black rocks.

'I wanna be an astronaut when I grow up,' said Gary. Everyone laughed, because no one from Greenheys School ever became an astronaut or anything on the telly, even if Mr Boyle said. Mr Boyle was the headmaster. He came about two years ago. He looked like Ken Barlow, only he had a mole on his left cheek. Mr Clark, the old headmaster, had died during the summer. He got married whilst on holiday and had a heart attack on his wedding night. So for three glorious weeks Greenheys was headmaster-free. Mrs Lodge, the deputy, didn't like to use the cane, so life was a riot until Mr Boyle arrived. He was kicked out of his last school after he hung a third year with his own shoelaces for chewing a Bazooka Joe in class, Carl said. So when Mr Boyle revealed his new plans for the school, no one laughed or made fun, not even the teachers.

And now, two years later, with a choir that sang carols at Manchester Cathedral, an orchestra of xylophones, glockenspiels and tambourines that brought the house down at the inter-school music festival at the Free Trade Hall and the annual Christmas party to Belle Vue Circus, James was sure of one thing: he didn't like Mr Boyle. They even had an assembly for Martin Luther King. Everyone sang 'We Shall Overcome' all day, and Mr Boyle had tears in his eyes, but James couldn't see why. How could he give you the slipper for fighting one minute, then blubber like a baby the next?

James didn't like Mr Boyle, but he hated Miss Young, really really hated Miss Young. She hated him too. He knew, because she'd said so. 'He will not do as he's told, Mrs Phillips,' she said to Mum, even though Mr Mackenzie wanted thirty Playtex bras done before five o'clock. 'Just because he's in the school orchestra he thinks he's mister high and mighty. I hear you're moving house, Mrs Phillips. Ashton-under-Lyne, James says. You must be very pleased.'

Mum went to see Mr Boyle afterwards but she didn't tell James. She gave him a bob for fish 'n' chips instead.

So by the time of the men on the moon, the whole school was well prepared. Firstly, all classes would stop at the sound of the bell. Then, one by one, starting from the first years up to the fourth years, each class would line up in the hall. And on Mr Boyle's whistle, everyone would sit down in silence.

'And I mean silence, or it's back to class and a spelling test for everyone, do I make myself clear?'

'Yes Mister *Boyalle*.'

Then he would nod to Miss Ryan to switch on the telly at the front of the hall. Greenheys Girls never lost a rounders match that year and the football team won five-nil in the schools' final. Still, no one from Greenheys would ever become an astronaut, even if Mr Boyle said over and over again.

When singing 'In the Bleak Midwinter' the right way to say iron was *eye-ron eye-ron eye-ron*. Mr Boyle made you practise over and over again until you had nightmares. He would clap his hands and stamp his feet until the floorboards shook.

'No one is leaving this room until everyone gets it right.'

They had to wait for Michael, and he did get it right eventually, but not until tears and snot ran down his face, and Cynthia was sent for a box of tissues from the staff room. By the time of the concert at Manchester Cathedral they'd got it so right they could have made a record. But they didn't. They didn't have their picture taken for the *Manchester Evening News* either. Mr Boyle had insisted. 'No,' he told the reporter, and everyone was really disappointed, but no one said.

Mr Boyle had killed a pupil by shouting so loud her eardrums burst and water poured out, Cynthia said. Despite this, he allowed James to stay home to take care of Mum as she lay moaning in bed after the holiday of a lifetime to the West Indies. When she got better, James was allowed to go on the school trip to Chester Zoo without paying. Mr Boyle also caned James for fighting with Michael on the back seat of the coach. So when James returned to school for the very last time before they moved to Ashton-under-Lyne, Mr Boyle said: 'I think it's for the best in the long run, Mrs Phillips. I try very hard, but there's only so much I can do.'

Which James didn't understand one bit. When he saw Mrs Rowbottom, his teacher in the infants, through the window of another class, she waved to him, and he waved back, even though he would never forgive her for getting married when she was Miss Mather, the greatest teacher in the world.

Anything else and it would be dead boring, sitting cross-legged on freezing cold floorboards with teachers along the side to block all possible routes of escape. Polar bears in a snowstorm. You couldn't understand what they said either. Just bleeps, scratches and James Burke getting overexcited. And when Neil Armstrong stepped on to the moon, James could have sworn he was going back up the ladder.

Still, it was better than lessons, any day.

twenty-three

'The Mash Potato's a dance, Aunty Mary, honest. No, you don't eat it – not even with gravy.'

'A four-four beat with a beat and a what?' said James.

'With a half beat hesitation,' said Aunty Mary, followed by a twirl as if to prove the point. 'Watch my feet,' and she went on to dance exactly like the Carmen Miranda dance from last Sunday's afternoon matinée on the telly but without the fruit. 'A four-four beat with a half beat hesitation, a four-four beat with a half beat hesitation, watch me feet, see how they move to the beat, a four-four beat and a half beat hesitation, a four-four beat...'

'... and a half beat hesitation,' danced James.

'Yes, that's it,' said Aunty Mary. 'I think you've got it, I think you've got it.' Then they both continued to dance exactly like the Carmen Miranda dance from last Sunday's afternoon matinée on the telly and still no fruit. 'A four-four beat with a half beat hesitation, a four-four beat with a half beat hesitation,' and they would've gone on dancing the South American way forever and ever amen if they'd had coconut and palm trees or even the men in the frilly shirts and maracas but unfortunately there was none of that, only a pile of rotting wood on the grass.

'Why on earth did you promise the man you'd make a fence from this lot?' said Aunty Mary.

'Mr Henderson said he'd give me a lemon fudgesicle if I did,' said James. 'They cost two dollars and if I did the fence he'd give me a dollar.' James picked up an old rusty tool box.

Aunty Mary sighed. 'Some people should be shot, promising little boys a pack of lies.'

'He wasn't telling lies, he gave me a dollar to start off with and he'll give me the next dollar when I've finished.' And James took out the coin from his pocket to show to Aunty Mary, which she took from his hands and bent with her teeth.

'I don't think you'll see him again. Oh James, what have I told you about talking to strangers. I mean, you don't know him from Adam.'

'Adam, who's Adam?'

'Exactly.'

'Mr Henderson, he's called Mr Henderson,' said James. 'Me dad told me about him.' And James continued like he was telling a story from memory so that if he didn't say it fast enough he'd forget it for ever. '. . . and Dad said Mr Henderson taught him how to be a carpenter because Mr Henderson needed a lot of work doing to his house and Mr Henderson couldn't teach his own son to be a carpenter because he was too busy doing his homework so he could be a big shot lawyer in the States.'

'So he taught your father carpentry?' said Aunty Mary as she inspected the tool box. In it was a hammer with only half a handle, and a tray full of rusty nails.

'Oh what am I going to do, Aunty Mary?'

'Might just as well make the most of it, James. Where did he say he wanted the fence putting up?'

'All around there, see?' And James pointed to the house in front of them. 'He says it must be done by this evening or else he won't give me the other dollar.'

'By this evening, eh? We're goner need some help,' said Aunty Mary as she took out a frying pan from her bag. 'Now run off home and bring me back a pack of sausages.'

'Now?'

'Yes, now.'

'What kind?'

'What do you mean, what kind? Just sausages, silly.'

'Pork, beef, Cumberland, Irish Link, skinless, I like skinless, they haven't any skin, sausages with herbs, sausages without, sausages ...' and James went on and on. There wasn't a lot James didn't know about sausages with Dad working at Wall's sausages ever since he got off the plane from the West Indies all those years ago before he met Mum. Not that Aunty Mary wanted to know about that. She'd had enough of James and all his sausages.

'Oh James, just a packet with eight in, okay? Ask your mother first. Tell her I'll pay her when I get back ... whoops, sorry, I forgot.'

'It's all right, Aunty Mary,' said James. 'I can wash the dishes for a few nights.'

'If I'm not here when you get back just follow the fence, okay?'

twenty-four

'Thank God it's Clarence Bailey. For a while I thought it was someone else. No, James, don't ask.'

The windows on Aunty Mary's house had been boarded up since last night. Big wooden planks over every one, even the upstairs. The front-room window had long since been broken so the board didn't make much difference, apart from keeping the cold out. The man from the council must've come in the middle of the night because the next morning the broken glass was gone. And while he was at it, the man from the council must have also painted SOLD over their FOR SALE sign in big bold letters. So now it was safe enough to stand in front of Aunty Mary's house and gossip, exactly like Mum and Mrs Jackson were doing as James looked on from a safe enough distance to run in case Mum made him go with her to the supermarket when she had finished talking with Mrs Jackson.

'You're joking,' said Mum. 'I don't believe you. Dead bodies, no way!'

'I'm telling you, Veronica, it's true. Three of them. Two men and a little girl, that's what I heard,' said Mrs Jackson.

'Oh yeah? Who said?'

'Does it matter? You know what these white people are like. Crazy.'

'Oh, Elseva, please.'

'I never did trust that woman. Craziest one of the lot if you ask me.'

'Oh not Mary,' said Mum. 'She was lovely. Always said hello, always had a smile on her face.'

'That's what I mean. Always smiling. I tell you, crazy woman.'

'Anyway, it's not good to speak ill of the dead.'

'I'm telling you, girl, crazy, the lot of them, you'll see.'

'Maybe so.'

'Well, Veronica, so long as you realise what you're letting yourself in for.'

'Yes, well,' said Mum, and then she looked away like she couldn't think of an answer.

'Still,' said Mrs Jackson, 'I wonder sometimes if we should move, you know.'

'Because of Grace?'

'Oh girl, don't talk to me about Grace. I tell you, Veronica. God give me strength.'

'It's not as if she's the first one to get herself pregnant. I should know.'

And Mrs Jackson nodded because everyone knew about Mum being pregnant with Felicia when she was still at school because Mum made sure she told anyone who didn't know. 'Yes, I know, Veronica, but still. It was different for us back *home*.'

'You can say that again.'

'Oh boy, wait till I tell you. You'll never guess?'

'Go on then, who?'

'Clarence.' And Mrs Jackson laughed like she'd said something really funny.

'What, Clarence, Clarence Bailey?'

'Clarence, yeah. I couldn't believe it neither.'

'Clarence? Little Clarence Bailey?'

'He's not so little now.'

'Little Clarence Bailey, eh? I take it he don't do the paper round no more?'

'It's not funny,' said Mrs Jackson.

'I know, but even so. Little Clarence Bailey. So what does Thomas say?'

'Girl, don't talk to me about Thomas. Oh boy. Thomas won't even let the girl in the house. Not after what she said. I tell you, the girl has no respect. He says he'll kill her next time he sees her. She's at her aunt's down Claremont Road. She's not coming back till she learns some respect, I tell you.'

'The girls today. They talk big and everything but look at them, eh? Just as stupid as we were. When I got pregnant with Felicia. Oh boy. Mama beat me every day for a whole week.'

'Oh Veronica, don't talk to me about beating, that's what started it in the first place. She threatened to call the police.'

'What??'

'After he slapped her. I mean, of course he slapped her. He's her father, for Christ sake. Honest truth, Veronica, I'm not joking. Call the police, she said. Boy, I had to jump on top of Thomas in case he killed her right there and then. He would've you know, you know what Thomas is like. The police, can you believe it?'

Mum and Mrs Jackson shook their heads at the same time like they were sisters.

'Good job you haven't a phone,' said Mum. Then they both started to laugh like they couldn't keep it in no more. And they went on laughing even when it wasn't funny any more. Then Mrs Cairns joined them from the other side of the road to ask them what was so funny and when they told her she started laughing too. Then Mrs Smith popped round the corner and soon she was laughing too and then Mrs Jones stuck her head out of the front window and before long they were all laughing and crying at the same time like grown-ups did when they laughed for too long.

twenty-five

'*Ooh*, you're right, James. The next one is short.'

James didn't actually rub his eyes but he may just as well have done because what was once a pile of rotting planks was now a freshly made up fence that went all the way round Mr Henderson's house and yard. And not only that, it also broke off and continued down the lane and disappeared over the hill. On closer inspection it looked a job very well done. Each plank was cut the same size, as wide as a big man's hand and as long as a cricket bat. And every single plank had been whitewashed to a gloss finish. James noticed a piece of paper sticking to one of the posts.

Follow the fence. Don't forget the sausages or else I'll send you back.

Love and Kisses, Aunty Mary.

James looked over the horizon. The fence seemed to go

on forever and ever amen. He could've sworn there wasn't that much wood and there had only been one box of rusty nails. But then nothing with Aunty Mary surprised him any more.

'What on earth do you want with a packet of sausages?' Mum had asked as she gave him a pack of Irish Links from the new fridge for the new house in Ashton-under-Lyne. James had already worked out an answer.

'Do you want me to lie?' he said, and when Mum said no, all he had to say was: 'Then I won't say nothing.'

So Mum had no choice but to hand over the sausages from out of the brand new fridge for their new house in Ashton-under-Lyne.

And as James followed the fence as instructed he made a note to remind himself to tell Aunty Mary about the new fridge for the new house in Ashton-under-Lyne that made blackcurrant ice cubes and stopped the mice from eating the pork pies. He looked back. Mr Henderson's house seemed a long way back but in front of him the fence went on and on and on. Then he remembered he hadn't asked Mr Henderson for the dollar so he could buy a lemon fudgesicle. He made another note to remind himself to ask Mr Henderson on his way back from wherever the fence led to.

twenty-six

'A colour telly now, is it? Do what you like, I'm past caring.'

They started out as a bunch of houses built a thousand years ago when there were no coloured people about. St Bees Street, Fairlawn Road, Monton Street, Moss Lane East. James knew these roads by heart. He'd passed them often enough on the way to church. St Bees, the houses with four floors and a cellar with no windows. Carl lived at Number 2 with his mum, dad and ten brothers and sisters. He was the youngest, so he had his own bedroom. James didn't know anyone with their own bedroom, not even Mum and Dad. It was Carl that James first heard it from.

'We're goner have a brand new house in the sky,' he said.

No one believed him, but no one said anything because his sister was the Cock of Greenheys. But when James went to church the next Sunday, he couldn't go the normal route because of the bulldozers, cranes and barbed-wire fences.

They were still there next week, but this time there were no houses. Like a bomb had exploded. A winter wonderland of bricks, dirt and old shopping trolleys. There was even an old abandoned broken-down car, just right for being Jim Clark. But when he returned the next week the car was gone and instead there were men in police uniforms and captain hats.

'Clear off you cheeky bugger.'

It was like a gigantic jigsaw puzzle in slow motion, one block on top of the other. First there were the big holes dug deep into the ground, big enough to bury a boat in. Then there were the big planks of iron stuck into those holes, a hundred feet high. James kept his distance just in case he accidentally touched them and knocked them over. He had his excuses ready just in case.

'I was at Everton's all day playing Ludo, honest.'

The next week the big iron planks had been partially covered by big flat thin walls of plaster with square holes in it, for the windows or something. James would have stayed longer, only *H. R. Puf-n-stuff* was on the telly in five minutes.

James didn't go for a while after that. After Mum and Aunty Vernice fell out they changed church. It was okay at the new church even though they didn't read stories from the Bible or play the tambourine. And after a while they stopped going to that one too. And that would have been the end of it when Carl entered the class in a brand new duffel coat. 'Guess what, we've got a new house, and we didn't have to move to no Ashton-under-Lyne neither.'

No one would have believed it only he invited James round to see for himself.

James almost fell over when he saw Carl's sister using a posh glass to drink water from the tap. It was exactly like the ones Mum kept in the china cabinet for special occasions like Christmas or a visitor from the West Indies. And there they were, Carl, his sister and James on the balcony of their new apartment overlooking a park with swings and roundabouts and a launderette for mothers to do their washing. It was Carl's sister that called it an *apartment*. 'Like in America,' she said, whilst sticking out her little finger on the hand she held the glass with.

'It's great, isn't it,' said Carl. And James had to agree, even though it didn't have a tree.

They were so high up that everything below looked like toys, Chad Valley toys in the posh department store in Piccadilly. Chad Valley and Raleigh. Those words were magic to James. Magic in his dreams, until now. The Chad Valley toys of buildings, houses, streets with lamp-posts, garages and car parks, where you could push your Dinky toy car up along the rank of three floors stopping off for two-pennies-worth of petrol. Once a year, Christmas shopping in Piccadilly. They couldn't afford anything in the posh department store, but it cost nothing to look, and dream. And now Carl was living in one, here, right here in Moss Side, and when James got home he would tell his mum and dad to come and have a look even though it didn't have its own tree. There were still dreams of Raleigh bikes with a hundred gears and seats as sharp as razors. But there was lots of time for that one to come true. Besides, he was only nine.

'You can see for miles around and at night all the streets and houses light up like the London Palladium,' said Carl.

'That's nice!' James replied, even though it was him that

had told Carl about the London Palladium Show in the first place.

A lift that went up when you pressed a button, a bathroom and toilet with no brown stains and taps that had hot water already, furniture so brand new the settee was covered in plastic. And as for the kitchen, James couldn't believe anything could be so clean and sparkly white. You had to wear goggles just to turn the tap. There was also hot air from the grilles in the walls.

'Just switch this switch and the heat comes on.' And it did too, like a hot breath on a cold day. 'No need for coal fires or anything. Bet your new house in Ashton don't have one.'

James wasn't about to bet anything. Betting was bad, Dad said. Dad said betting was so bad, you could lose all your money or even the shirt off your back. And James wasn't about to lose his brand new bri-nylon white shirt to no one, especially Carl.

Carl was really enjoying himself now. There was no way James could match that, even with caterpillars in the tree. But that didn't matter, because there was something else which was even more magnificent than anything he'd seen so far. Much better than the lift, the thin walls so you could hear everything the neighbours said, even better than the little people waiting for the toy buses. James had heard about them but had never seen one before. No one he knew had seen one, not even Mr Boyle. But there before his very eyes, like a shrine in a temple, was a colour television showing Bugs Bunny cartoons. James wanted to fall to his knees in prayer, only he didn't want to muck up the shagpile carpet. James's only concern now was to get Carl to invite him for dinner sometime, on a Sunday afternoon when *H. R. Puf-n-stuff* was on. He would even let Carl come top in Spelling.

twenty-seven

'Gosh, this is more fun than the war.'

Brimstone Hill was the hill where the British defeated the French with a bunch of cannons and took over the island of St Kitts. They built a fort so the cannons would have somewhere to stay in case the French decided to come back. All that was a long time ago when Francis Drake was still alive. Now nothing was left but a few rusty cannons and a flat hill top which was ideal for picnics on bank holidays. Which was why Aunty Mary asked James for a packet of sausages in the first place.

'You can't get them up here for love nor money, it's just like the war. I'll bring tea and cakes, it'll be like old times.'

And it was, almost. Apart from being on top of Brimstone Hill. He'd only brought the one packet, it had took him all his effort to bring that one. Mum wouldn't stop pestering. 'Heaven knows what you want them for.'

'You always tell me not to lie, so I'm saying nothing.'

With that there was nothing Mum could do but hand

over a packet of Irish Links. But not before having the final say. 'Fill the coal bucket every day for two weeks and I'll think about it.'

Aunty Mary had the frying pan heating on an oil heater ready before James arrived and now the sausages were sizzling in the pan just like an advert on the telly. Soon the whole of Brimstone Hill was filled with the smell of sausages sizzling in their own fat and the noise was so loud you could've heard it at the bottom of the hill which was about a hundred feet below on to some rocks. Aunty Mary was over the moon. 'This is heaven,' she said as she jabbed and prodded the sausages with a fork. 'Pass us the plate will you?'

That was the third plate she'd filled with sausages but he'd only brought one packet and there were only eight sausages to one pack. And still the pan was sizzling full. 'Hope there's enough for everyone,' said Aunty Mary.

'For everyone?'

'They'll be back in a minute. You don't think I did the fence all by myself. Make yourself useful and pass me another plate.'

And sure enough, three trucks came over the hill each full of people dressed up like they were going to church.

Mary looked at her watch. 'Right on time.' Then she handed James the fork. 'Take care of these while I powder me nose.'

James was relieved Aunty Mary didn't tell him who she wanted the sausages for. If she had, well ... 'I can't get that many,' he would've said. 'There isn't that many sausages in the whole wide world.'

And he would've been right too. There must have been a whole village there, all of them in their Sunday best because coloured people always dressed in their best whenever they went out. By now there was a real party atmosphere, it could've been a carnival only there was no steel band. Aunty Mary and her endless plates of sausages were the centre of attraction.

'Single file or no one gets served.'

Everyone laughed because everyone knew the English were crazy if the letters from relatives were anything to go by. Even so, they formed a queue because it would've been bad manners not to. And everyone was calling her Aunty Mary by now. Not that she minded, she was loving every minute of it, sleeves rolled up, cheerfully red-faced, dishing out sausages on sticks by the five thousand.

'It's just like the war. Seconds anyone?' Mary looked up to the skies. 'Looks like rain.' Then she noticed James wasn't eating. 'What's up James, lost your appetite?'

Ever since they'd arrived, James saw that the people were dressed strange even for St Kitts. It was like one of those really old black and white photos from Aunty Vernice's album, the one she kept in the china cabinet. From when she was a little girl, she said. The whole of the village had been in the picture, it had been taken just before they'd set off for the annual picnic on Brimstone Hill.

'You look as if you've seen a ghost, James.'

If Aunty Vernice's stories were true then she was right, or she would be once the rains started, and the crowds would rush for cover to shelter from the rain, and the rain poured down and they pushed and jostled each other so much that some of them were pushed off the hill down on to the rocks below.

'They'd been up all night ironing their hair straight. They didn't want their hair to get wet. You know what it's like when it gets wet, it goes frizzy again,' Aunty Vernice had said on one of many visits to her house when James had asked why.

Aunty Mary would have none of it.

'Absolute hogwash! Why would anyone throw themselves off this beautiful hill?' she said as she pointed to where the hill dropped down to the rocks below. And everyone laughed because no one was about to drop off any hill, especially when there were lots of sausages left.

James didn't know what to do; the clouds were really dark by now and looked like they were about to burst any moment. 'She wouldn't lie, she wouldn't make up something like that, would she?' said James, tugging at Aunty Mary's apron, urging her to get away from here as soon as possible. 'She promised to take me home when she wins the pools.'

Aunty laughed as the sizzling pan spat fat as if to prove the point. 'Exactly,' she said. 'Thirds anyone?'

And everyone else laughed too because they knew the young woman who called herself Vernice. She hadn't been the same since she started courting that half-caste boy who worked on the railways.

And the rains did come down, a really heavy downpour, even worse than in Moss Side. But no one seemed to mind, they were too busy having fun and queuing up for more sausages. Also, they had come prepared for the rain by wearing plastic headscarves sent over by relatives in England. So the only things that fell over the hill were the stones thrown by James. It was a new game he'd just made up: how long it would take for the stones to hit the rocks below.

'One, two, three, four? . . . five??'

twenty-eight

'I *really* think you should stay awake for this one, Aunty Mary.'

Now this one was a really weird one, even for James. It started off the same way as some of the others. One minute he was in his bedroom listening to Aunty Mary telling him her life story. The next he and Aunty Mary were on a settee in the middle of Cadogen Street, helping themselves to tea and biscuits whilst watching bits of Aunty Mary's life story being acted out right there in front of her front door. Only the important bits, mind you, anything else would've been just too weird, even for James. Even so, James knew everything would sort itself in the end. Besides, he was in safe hands with Aunty Mary even if she couldn't make her mind up whether to laugh or cry.

It hadn't taken him long to guess who the little girl stealing money from the milk bottles was. It was Miriam when she was a little girl. She looked a lot like the scruffy little girl who had stolen James's money only Miriam's hair was long and brassy, even as a little girl. Recognising Jake as a young man was much harder. James had always thought it was Arthur who was in the photo on Aunty Mary's mantelpiece. How was he to know it was Jake all along and there was no such person as Arthur, but that was another story.

Everything began straightforward enough. James was having a nightmare at the time. The Sister Ruth nightmare, the one where a lady in a black dress, black hair and black eyes chased him through the jungle with an axe in her hand. James has had that nightmare ever since he saw Sister Ruth on a Sunday matinée a few weeks ago. Sister Ruth was the nun who decided she'd had enough and didn't want to be a nun no more. So she put on a black dress, high heel shoes and lipstick and tried to push the Deborah Kerr nun off a really high cliff. But Sister Ruth fell off instead of the Deborah Kerr nun which was a good job really. Even so, James had been having the Sister Ruth nightmares ever since. Regularly as clockwork too, every Friday night in fact, after a fish and chips supper and chocolates brought by Dad after work. So James was really relieved when Aunty Mary appeared before he'd had a chance to wet the bed.

'This one's for me,' she said. 'It's about time I had one, don't you think?'

'Had one what?' said James.

'No fireworks I'm afraid. You may find it a bit soppy in parts.'

'Like *Panorama*?'

'Nothing like *Panorama*, silly,' said Aunty Mary. 'Mind you, I'd better give a run down of the schedule, just in case.' So James sat up, his feet folded like waiting for Mr

Boyle to finish a really long prayer in assembly.

She called it *The Aunty Mary Show*, and under no circumstances was there to be any music whatsoever.

'What, no music?' said James.

'Not even Bing Crosby,' said Aunty Mary.

She said it was to be in Cadogen Street and they would have a really good view in the middle of the road.

'You mean like the Grace one?' said James.

'Not exactly like the Grace one, but close enough,' said Aunty Mary.

Then they suddenly appeared in the middle of Cadogen Street all ready and waiting for the show to begin. On the coffee table was a pot full of tea and a large plate of assorted biscuits.

'Chocolate digestive? Custard creams?' said Aunty Mary.

'Yes please,' said James.

The Aunty Mary Show had been going on for a while now, okay enough so far, even though James would have added a few little touches here and there, just for effects like. For a start there had to be a plane crash, any good story had to start with a plane crash. A really big bang with lots of fire so there was nothing left but a really big cinder pitch, so big you could play two games of football and not get in each other's way. Then everything would be perfect, just perfect, for starting again like it was the first day back after the summer holidays. Thankfully there would be no one on the ground at the time of the crash because they were at school or work or on the social. There would be no survivors on the plane, of course, which was very sad but there you go.

'You can't crack an omelette without making eggs,' said

Aunty Mary, which made far more sense than it should have done considering her false teeth had just fallen out. She was laughing at the young man in a Brylcreem suit who was banging on the front door like he wanted to break it down. If James wasn't mistaken, the young man looked a lot like a young Jake only the young man had hair.

'Let me in,' screamed the young man. 'I know you're in there, Mary. I can smell baking.'

Aunty Mary was still laughing even though James couldn't see what was so funny.

'I meant what I said, I can't live without you,' said the young man. 'I love you, Mary, I love you.'

And with that, Aunty Mary fell off the settee and collapsed to the floor. 'Oh my,' she laughed, 'it's funnier than Laurel and Hardy.'

'Was he always like this?' asked James

'Only the once, thank goodness,' said Aunty Mary as she picked herself off the floor. 'Mavis, his wife, had refused to make his favourite, steak and kidney pudding with mushy peas and gravy. I mean, James, what was a girl to do. Run to his beck and call every time he came knocking with a bunch of flowers? I should cocoa. He should've thought of that when he married her, daft sod.'

And before you could say bobs your uncle Aunty Mary was well into the story of how Jake and her were really really really good friends and how they would have stayed that way if she hadn't gone away to the war to be a nurse. 'Not that I'm complaining, mind you. I had a good war and everything. I know I shouldn't say it but I had a really good war.'

And *The Aunty Mary Show* went on for a bit longer,

and again James wanted to make changes but what could he do, it wasn't his show. If James had his way then there would be fireworks right now. Bangers, rockets, Catherine wheels, sparklers even. Anything that went whizz bang pop and made you put your hands over your ears. And music too, you had to have music no matter what Aunty Mary said, Glenn Miller especially. Well you had to, it was the war you know. 'I told him to wait, I did. Ooh, he was a daft bugger. I told him, "It'll be over by Christmas, you mark my words," I said.' And when James asked who was Arthur then, Aunty Mary said it saved a lot of confusion calling him Arthur which made James even more confused. Even so, he thought it best not to ask, just in case.

Now the next bit was just too weird, even for James. It should've started all over again, it was in a right mess. For a start, there would be a three minute warning, of course. A news flash on BBC1 followed by a front page in the *Manchester Evening News*, just in case. There would be a plane crash of course, but this time instead of the passengers there would be a large can of Esso Blue on every seat. The pilot would be the only person on board but it was okay because he lived alone by himself in a cottage in Abergavenny. And this time the whole of Moss Side would be burnt to a cinder as well as Whalley Range and even Chorlton-cum-Hardy. And this time to make sure that no one was around at the time there would be a Billy Smart Circus at Belle Vue extra specially. Yes, if only James had his way and started all over again. But he couldn't, of course. It was Aunty Mary's show – *THE AUNTY MARY SHOW* in big bright lights and as usual with Aunty Mary she had to do things her way come hell or high water, whatever that meant. So there they were, in the middle of Cadogen Street and dunking arrowroot biscuits in a cup of tea because all the nice ones had been eaten by then.

'Don't leave it in for long or else . . . see I told you,' said Aunty Mary trying hard to sound vexed. But James had only left it in because he was distracted by the little girl in a scruffy overcoat who was looking inside the milk bottles on the doorsteps and shaking them.

'Hey, that's the girl who stole me money.' And before James could run over and bash her brains in, Aunty Mary patted him on the shoulder.

'Whoa there, young man.'

So James sat back, determined to give the little girl a good piece of his mind once Aunty Mary's back was turned.

'Miriam was a scruffy little thing,' said Aunty Mary like she was wanting to cry but couldn't. 'She never did say where she came from, I never thought to ask. Look, she's at my door now. And I thought it was sparrows. Oh, James, if I'd known it was her I'd have left more than two bob.'

Just then Aunty Mary's front door opened and out stepped a young woman in a dressing gown and pink fluffy slippers.

'I was good looking back then, don't you think? No girdle neither.'

The little girl stood frozen to the spot like she'd been caught doing something naughty. She had, of course. The young woman smiled and held out her arms. Then both Aunty Mary and the young woman said the same thing at the same time.

'Come in out of the cold, dear. Don't worry, I won't bite.'

Oh no, thought James, this won't do, this just won't do. It had to start again, start all over again. It wouldn't matter whether it was a jumbo jet or an Olivia De Havilland biplane. It wouldn't matter neither if there were any passengers on board or not or if anyone just happened to be on the ground at the time. It wouldn't matter at all in the slightest bit whatsoever because when the two hydrogen bombs on the plane went off then oh brother. There would be no choice then, absolutely no choice whatsoever and everyone, absolutely everyone would have to start over and over again. Then everyone would know what it was like to have to start all over again and have to move to a brand new semi-detached house with a front lawn and a garage and not another black face for miles, Dad said.

twenty-nine

'Can't be me, inside that coffin? Gosh, I've lost weight.'

'Darling, Darling.'

It was always the same when shopping with Mum. She'd meet someone she knew and then she'd have to stop and talk. Mum knew absolutely everyone when she went out shopping so it was surprising she ever got any shopping done. And now was no different even though it was only the ironmonger's on Moss Lane East with Charlie, the man behind the counter who dressed like a woman when he felt like it. Today he was wearing a white frock with orange flowers, a brown pullover and on his hands were a pair of black woolly gloves with the fingertips cut off so everyone could see his green covered fingernails. He also had far too much lipstick on for his own good which was a shame really but there you go, Mum said.

'Come over here, darling, you're looking *good*.' And they pretended to kiss each other on the cheek like they really meant it.

'Long time no see,' Mum said even though she'd been in for a box of matches only yesterday.

Charlie was just as bad. 'Where *did* you get those gloves, darling?'

'Marshall Ward's.'

'What part of Piccadilly is that then, dear?' And they laughed even though everyone knew Marshall Ward was a catalogue that came through the letterbox.

It was the same every time. If it wasn't the gloves it would be something else. The way Mum plaited her hair, how she walked, her perfume, lipstick, anything, so long as Charlie could talk to Mum like they were the best of friends. Charlie could talk a lot for a man, even for one who dressed like a woman. He didn't need a bottle of rum or two pints of Davenport's Brown Ale or wrestling on the telly neither. James liked him a lot even though his friends threw stones at Charlie from the school yard during last Tuesday's afternoon playtime. 'Aunty Man,' Carl had called Charlie. James had enough aunts to last him a lifetime so another one wouldn't make much difference whatsoever. When Carl tried to explain, James was even more confused.

'Do it with a man, do what with a man?' And everyone laughed and they called him an Aunty Man too. Then Mrs Ryan sent Carl and James to Mr Boyle for the slipper.

But that was last Tuesday and luckily Charlie had forgotten about the stone throwing because he gave James a handful of Mo-Jos from the big jar on the counter even though the shop was an ironmonger's. If James had known they would be a long time talking then he would've took two handfuls instead of the usual one.

'Meet my *mother*,' said Charlie to Mum as he hugged the lady who was with him behind the counter. The lady said

Hello dear I've heard so much about you, even though she looked younger than Charlie. She looked young enough to be his girlfriend in fact, or even his wife but that was impossible because Aunty Men weren't allowed to marry, Carl said.

'Didn't I tell you she was a beauty,' said Charlie, but James didn't think she looked that good until he realised his mistake and Mum started to giggle like a little girl.

'He's impossible isn't he,' said Mum.

'Isn't he just,' said Charlie's mother and she kissed Charlie on the forehead.

You know what it's like when you do something or hear something that you've done before. A bird whistling, something off the telly, being chased down the road by next-door's dog. You know what it's like. You know you've done it before, exactly the same. Yesterday perhaps, a week ago, a year even, or maybe another lifetime. That was exactly how it felt to James right there and then with Mum, Charlie and Charlie's mum in Charlie's shop, the ironmonger's shop at the corner of Moss Lane East and Fernleaf Street in Moss Side Manchester in the late 1960s. Exactly like the last time, you know, **the last time with the wah-wah trumpets without Shirley Bassey never mind James Bond, and the long black car with Aunty Mary's coffin in the back.**

Charlie's laughter brought James back to earth with a bang.

'I use a small paintbrush, you know, like the kiddies at school,' said Mum as she mimicked a painting action over her lips. '*Vwola*, no smudges.'

Sometimes there'd be others in the shop, and they'd talk like a bunch of girls too. But it was only Charlie who dressed like one. He didn't fool anyone, though, not even the police. They would call round occasionally and take him in for a little chat. 'To keep me in line,' said Charlie, and then he laughed even though he looked like he didn't want to. And if James was listening he wouldn't have laughed neither because as everyone knew, keeping in line outside Broadfield Road Baths wasn't easy, especially when. Errol was thumping you in the back. But James wasn't listening as his mind was on other things. Because even though they were still in Charlie's ironmonger's, as far as James was concerned **there might just as well be wah-wah trumpets and water flowers right up to the window sill, thank you very much.**

It was funny how you remember something much later on that you don't remember at the time it happened. The **small things**, so **little** and **titchy** you couldn't help but miss it at the time but when you looked back you wonder **how the hell** could you have missed that one, for heavens sake. That was how it was **with the wah-wah trumpets without James Bond and Jake standing on the other side of the road at Aunty Mary's funeral as her coffin was brought from the house. Sobbing away like his heart had broke in two, not noticing the pouring rain as it soaked his Brylcreem suit. And there on top of the coffin was a big bunch of flowers arranged to spell out MARY in big capital letters. It was so big you could see it from the upstairs bedroom across the other side of the street. Even the birds high up in the sky couldn't help but notice.**

Both Charlie and Charlie's mother were well into their stride by now. 'We wouldn't have met if it wasn't for Mary,' said Charlie's mother.

'Oh yes, I remember her exact words. *You'll see,* she said, *the police will leave you alone once you're married.* She was right too.'

'I made an honest man out of you.'

'Who you calling a *man*?'

And they both laughed and kissed like a couple of school girls.

The people-in-black. Of course. It was as clear as another repeat of *Bonanza*. The three women wearing black skirts, a hat and a net covering their faces. He would never of recognised Miriam, Charlie and his mum, never in a million years. No way could he have known it was Charlie who was holding on to Miriam to stop her falling to the floor, not even in another million years, not even in kingdomcome.

'There wasn't anything anyone could've done. You know what Miriam was like. Once she put her mind to something that was it.'

'How could she, I mean how could she? I tell you, it makes me want to, I wanna kill her myself when I think about Heather and Louise.'

'I think the least said about that woman the better.' And both Charlie and his mother folded their arms like they'd had enough.

And if anyone could hear what Mum was thinking then they would've heard the following.

'What did you expect anyway, no surprise to me really, that's what you people are like but hey what the hell, it's not my country.'

If Aunty Mary had opened up her coffin and looked out Aunty Mary would've liked the dress that Charlie wore at her funeral. A long black dress suited Charlie, it made him look graceful and almost lady-like for a change.

Much better than the mini-skirts and black stockings he usually wore.

'It's Heather and Louise I feel sorry for, poor kids.'

'Heather's old enough to look after herself, it's Louise I feel sorry for, poor kid. She's having to stay with her aunty.'

'I thought there weren't no relatives?'

'One of Mary's friends.'

Then Charlie and his mother said *Ahh* at the same time.

They could've been three sisters, Charlie, his mother and Miriam. Charlie being the oldest of course, the unmarried one who stayed at home to look after Mother. Charlie's mother the middle sister, the serious one who had married young and had three kids, and Miriam the youngest, the spoilt one, Daddy's favourite. The one who was always out dancing and would come back late with her stockings torn.

'I was dead set on having it done you know, *the operation*. Been to the doctors and everything, I was that convinced I was. I tell you, Mary put me straight she did and in no uncertain terms as well. *Look here*, Mary said, the way she did, *Look here young man*. I was young then, those were the days.'

'Get on with it, oh he does go on sometimes,' shouted Mum and Charlie's mum at the same time.

'Anyway, like I said, Mary put me straight. *Look here*, she said. *Once it's gone there's no going back, you know. That's that. It's goodnight Vienna*,' said Charlie, still trying to be like Aunty Mary but sounding far too like a man even for Charlie. That didn't stop all three of them laughing like a bunch of idiots.

'*Goodnight Vienna, goodnight Vienna*. I tell you, our Mary – priceless.'

And soon all three of them were so out of control there was no making sense of them whatsoever. Mum was holding her chest like her girdle was too tight, Charlie's mum honked away like a sea-lion at Chester Zoo and as for Charlie, well, the way he clung on to the cash till you would think he was drowning.

Grown-ups were daft like that, thought James. Most of the time they'd be serious and boring. Then all of a sudden, without any warning and for no reason, that was it.

As Aunty Mary would say, it was goodnight Vienna.

thirty

'So tell me, James, how did your Aunty Vernice lose her finger?'

The ten foot snowman in front of Mrs Powell's was of no interest to James. Neither was the giant snowball as big as a big man that was rolling at a rate of knots towards him. He did a neat little side step just in case it didn't miss. No, all he was interested in was the snow all around, everywhere, as far as the eye could see. Last night on the telly, Burt Ford the weatherman said it would snow really deep but James didn't believe him as the snow in Moss Side was only as thin as skin on custard. Even when the wind blew hard in the night James thought at the very least there'd be a few bins blown over. So you can imagine his surprise when he opened the curtains and there outside the window was a winterwonderland straight off a Bing Crosby Christmas Special. In two seconds flat he'd brushed his teeth, combed his hair, fought with his sisters and eaten his cornflakes. Now he was having another breakfast, a gobful of crunched up snow. Snow three foot deep tasted different to the usual snow they had in Moss Side. For a start you could actually taste the snow and not bits of coal or tar or whatever was left on the street the night before. **And it tasted like the pictures of snow in the encyclopaedias in the front room, sparkling decorations of ice that tingled your tongue and made you glad to be alive. As far as James was concerned Cadogen Street could stay covered in snow like this forever and ever amen. And he would've told Aunty Mary too when she suddenly turned up from nowhere as usual but she had other things on her mind. So instead of saying hello and how are you, she cuffed James across the head.**

'You're late, you're late, for a very important date,' said Aunty Mary and she handed James a plastic bag which had in it a small glockenspiel exactly like the one he played in the school orchestra. 'If we run we might just make it for the last bit.'

James was used to Aunty Mary turning up unexpected like this but he had to make sure. 'Run where?' he asked.

'Alexandra Park, of course silly,' said Aunty Mary.

Alexandra Park was the park at the end of Claremont Road. On a normal day it was a five minute sprint even if you were the second fastest runner in the class. Not today though. Moss Side wasn't used to having three feet of snow. Besides, there were also other things that weren't the same. First of all, from what he could tell, there were cobbles under the snow instead of the usual tarmac, even off Princess Road. And the cars and buses had turned into horses and carriages and people were dressed like they'd just got off a George Formby film. The snow made the horses slip and slide all over the place whilst kids with buckets and shovels followed behind. The people on the pavement just stood there and laughed.

'Eee mother, they're off again,' they said, in their cloth caps, scarves and clogs, waiting for the signal to all join hands and parade down the street singing ♪With My Little Stick of Blackpool Rock♪

Not that Aunty Mary seemed to notice. She was too busy dragging James by the elbows. 'Spit spot, on the dot.' Then she looked at her watch. 'Oh my goodness.'

And James agreed but it wasn't because of the time. It was because a plane with two wings was about to land right there in front of them, in the middle of Princess Road. The plane skidded for a few yards, spraying snow on to the pavement and bystanders until finally it stopped and flipped on to its propellers in front of Yates's Wine Lodge. It was a good job there weren't any cars and buses too or else there would've been a right mess. Everyone rushed to the stricken plane as it lay in the snow. James ran up to join them which didn't please Aunty Mary one bit.

'It's always like this when you're in a hurry,' she said as she too rushed to join the crowd that had formed a neat circle. The pilot had got out by now, and was signing autographs and shaking hands. A queue had formed leading to the pilot, all ready with the pencils and books. James looked at Aunty Mary and she reached into her bag and took out an old black book with a pencil down the middle. 'I always have one ready for emergencies like this,' and she handed James an exercise book. 'Make sure he returns the pencil. The amount of times I've lost one because they forgot to give it back, I don't know . . .' But James didn't hear the last bit as he rushed to stand behind a man in a suit and bowler hat. The man looked at James and smiled.

'You can go in front of me, sonny. You're in a rush aren't you.'

'Thank you, Mister.'

And the man in the bowler hat didn't stop there. He took James by the hand and led him to the front. The people didn't seem to mind and smiled at James as he went past. But just in case, the man gave excuses. 'Sorry, he's in a hurry, important business, gangway.'

Eventually they reached the front of the queue, and there was the pilot looking a lot like Aunty Mary would have done if she was a young man and dressed in a pilot's uniform. The man in the bowler pushed James forward. 'Go on, he won't bite.'

The pilot looked up from signing and winked at James like they were the best of friends. 'Hello, little coloured boy, and what part of Africa are you from?'

'I'm not from Africa, I live over there.' James pointed down the road in the direction of what should have been the brewery but was now an open field with cows and dandelions.

'Yes, I know. I was just pretending.' And again he winked at James as he signed James's book with a flourish. James didn't have time to look at the signature as a hand grabbed his elbow.

'We haven't got time to chit chat young man, hurry along.' Aunty Mary dragged James off before he had a chance to ask the pilot if he was Aunty Mary's little brother. Which was just as well because the next minute a policeman had arrived and placed handcuffs on the pilot. Not that the crowd seemed to mind; they just clapped and threw their scarves and caps in the air.

'Hurrah,' they cheered. 'Good ol' Tommy Atkins.'

Aunty Mary was almost dragging James by now. 'I hope you remember the tune, young man,' she said.

'The tune?'

'Yes, the tune, the polish something or the other.'

' "The Polka".'

'Yes, that as well. Hurry James, it's no use getting cold feet now.'

'Cold feet?' said James. 'I got me shoes on, look.' And he stopped to point to his shoes.

'This isn't the time to play in the snow, young man, now hurry along before I take back what I said about you.'

'Take back?'

'I told them you were the best player in the school.'

'Oh Aunty Mary,' cried James, 'I said I was the second best. No one can play better than Cynthia, no one! That's the last time I tell you anything.'

'In for a penny, in for a nine bob note,' said Aunty Mary as they crossed Claremont Road just as a herd of cows came running down the road. It could have been straight off *Rawhide*, *Bonanza* or even *The High Chaparral*, but it wasn't. It was Claremont Road and it was exactly like when Aunty Mary was a little girl. James knew because she said so as they stood on the other side of the road by Seymour Mead's watching the stampeding herd go by. 'They're on the way to the abattoirs. My word, it brings it all back.' Then she looked at her watch. 'Three o'clock every Thursday, you could set your watch by them.'

The cows continued to run, some slipping in the snow and leaving manure in the road. Not that the passers by seemed to mind, they were too busy waiting for Gracie

Fields to jump out of Grimshaw's fish and chips shop in her apron and headscarf to lead in a rousing rendition of everybody's favourite, 'Sing As We Go'!

Over in the distance, in the middle of a cornfield, a band was playing. And from what James could make out the band was playing the same tune their school orchestra had played at the concert at the Free Trade Hall, 'The Polka'. And they'd just started so that meant in two minutes' time James was due to play his solo bit on the glockenspiel.

'Help, Mummy,' screamed James and he ran off in the direction of the bandstand.

'Don't worry about me, young man, you go right ahead,' shouted Aunty Mary. 'And remember, tripe's good meat if it's wiped well.'

'The Polka', or to give it its full title 'The Polish Polka'. It took three weeks to learn his bit on the glockenspiel, two weeks of Mr Boyle screaming down James and everyone else's face. He was good like that was Mr Boyle, he never had favourites, he screamed at everyone, especially if they got a note wrong. So when James reached the bandstand and the band-leader dressed like Sergeant Pepper said you've got ten seconds nine eight seven ... good luck, whilst still waving his baton, James wasn't the least bit worried because when you've had Mr Boyle losing his dentures through screaming just two inches away from your nose, well, everything else was a piece of cake. So in just five seconds flat James had mounted the glockenspiel on the table, replaced the loose keys back in the right holes, stuck on one of the beater's woolly heads with chewing gum, said hello to the rest of the band before the band-leader pointed to James to indicate it was his turn.

'Yoo hoo, cooeee, I'm over here,' shouted Aunty Mary from the comfort of a deck-chair with the rest of the audience who were all dressed like they were about to appear on *The Good Old Days*. Then she winked at James exactly like the pilot had done before and James wondered if maybe Aunty Mary had been a pilot in the war instead of a nurse. Or maybe she'd been both a pilot and a nurse at the same time. It wouldn't have surprised James in the least. Aunty Mary was clever like that.

The rest of James's piece was a blur of counting in time and striking the right notes, two three. He knew the tune so well he could play it with his eyes closed, but he didn't risk it in case Mr Boyle was in the audience. And just as it began it was over, James had done his bit and had sat down to catch his breath. As the trumpet player did his solo, the band-leader stepped down from the podium and sat next to James.

'Well done, James, excellent playing young man.'

'Thank you,' said James.

'This is a small present to show our appreciation.' And the band-leader handed James a small bottle. The bottle was the size of a small hip flask and it appeared to contain a clear liquid. 'I bet you're wondering what's in it,' said the band-leader, then he shook the bottle and the liquid turned brown.

'Wow,' said James, 'it's magic.'

'Chocolate,' said the band-leader as he handed James the bottle. 'Not too hard or the top might come off.' And when James shook the bottle the liquid turned yellow. 'Lemon cordial,' said the band-leader as he twiddled with his long moustache as if to prove the point. 'First shake chocolate, the next shake lemon and the final shake makes it clear again.' He was right too because when James shook it a final time the liquid went back to clear.

As he stepped back on to the podium the band-leader had one more piece of advice. 'I think this is what you've been looking for.' And before James could ask him what the hell was he talking about, the band-leader said one last thing. 'I can't help you with the rest of your journey, young man, but if you look all around you will find the answer underfoot.' Then the band-leader winked at James. You never know, thought James, with a few grey hairs, hairnet, pink slippers and night-gown, he could easily be Aunty Mary's long lost twin brother and no one would even notice, not even the milkman.

Normally, it would have been all right. James had gone that way lots of times. Out the main entrance on to Alexandra Road, cross over by the traffic lights where Claremont Road meets Princess Road and follow Princess Road until it turns into Raby Street and from there you couldn't miss Moss Lane East unless you were really stupid. Normally, that is, but this wasn't normal and as he approached a bunch of bushes with mangoes on the branches James wished he hadn't taken the short cut through the alley at the back of Westwood Road. The snow had melted long ago and all that was left was a carpet of lush green grass so springy you could walk in your bare feet and bounce up and down at the same time. It was a good job he'd been here before or else he really would've been worried. And as the grass underfoot turned into the lane that led up to Mr Orson's house in St Kitts in the West Indies, James remembered what the band-leader had said and went on his way hoping whatever he met wouldn't be too scary and give him nightmares.

If it was the end of the world it would've been the final record. On Radio 1, Radio Luxembourg or even Radio Caroline. There'd be no DJs left because they'd be long gone by now, to the place where DJs go to die. Wherever they were, James hoped they were as comfortable as the almost half-caste lady laying there on the leather settee in the front room of Mr Orson's house. She looked like she was asleep but if the stories were true then it was a sleep she would never wake up from. She had long straight shiny black hair and dribble dropped down the side of her mouth but thankfully it missed the head of the baby that was asleep in her arms. And James could see the lady laying there on the leather settee. Mum was right all along, her mum was very pretty, very pretty indeed. So pretty in fact that it was easy enough to fall head over heels in love with her and not eat your tea for ages.

The record wouldn't have to be a slow one to be sad. It could be a Phil Spector 'Wall of Sound' with a Motown bass and drum. But everyone would know it was a sad record even though it didn't say so on the label. You could even dance to it in a discotheque but you would know it was sad because no amount of shaking would wake up the almost half-caste lady because it was the kind of sleep that no one woke up from.

And if Mum's stories were true, the sleeping baby was Samuel, James's uncle, Mum's half-brother, which half James didn't know. The same Samuel who always made Mum cry when she was a little girl. He didn't have to do anything neither, he'd just stand there in the entrance or in the backyard, whenever Mum would go on her visits to see her little brother at his father's house. And it would always end with Mum bursting into tears for no reason and hugging and squeezing him like a long lost teddy bear.

The words wouldn't have to make any sense neither. As long as it made your chest go tight when you heard it and have to lie down on a leather settee. The singer didn't have to be American neither, or a woman, or coloured neither, but it would help.

Some said it was Mr Orson that killed Mum's mum. They said he'd caught her stealing from the pantry and he shouted at her so loud she dropped dead with blood running down her legs. Others, including Aunty Vernice, said it was the husband that did it. They said he treated her so badly, beating her till she was no longer almost half-caste, making her work while he stayed at home and let his mother cook for him, that in the end she decided maybe it wasn't such a bad idea to die after all because it had to be better than the life down here.

Yes, it had to be a sad song, only a sad song would do. And as the baby slept and the grandfather clock ticked away James hummed the words of the song because now was as right a time as any. Besides, it went well with the rest of Mum's story about her mother. A story of a woman who had a child by Mum's father but didn't marry the father because he was too black and a fisherman. But she couldn't go home to her own mother and sisters because the shame was too much so she decided to marry the first man who came along who luckily for her turned out to be a half-caste who worked in town at the bank but in the end it didn't matter because it was Mrs Orson that found Mum's mum in the living room of their house with a baby asleep in her arms even though she was only twenty-five years old.

The clock chimed one-fifteen and if Mum was right there'd be at least another hour before Mrs Orson would wake up from her midday nap and all hell would be let loose.

'I can't remember what she looked like,' said Mum that time in the sewing room when she told James the whole story for the first time. 'Your Aunty Vernice has some photos, I've heard. I'm sure your Aunt Vernice has her reasons for not showing me the photos. That's it, she must have her reasons.'

Then she told James that Aunty Vernice was also her mum's sister. 'So she's my aunty too,' Mum said.

James thought it was really groovy having the same aunty as your mum but now he wasn't so sure. And why hadn't Aunty shown Mum the photos. At the time he'd could imagine what she'd look like, she'd be in a white dress and would have a pink handbag strapped on to her elbow, looking into the camera with a tinted-on smile. The photo itself would have a gold-covered curvy outline, mounted in a silver mirrored frame. It would have a special place above the telly so everyone could see. But Mum didn't have the photo so it was destined to spend the rest of its life in an envelope inside the back pocket of an old pink handbag that was wrapped up in an old white confirmation dress which in turn was packed with a lot of other junk into a suitcase with a jammed lock and the key lost and the suitcase itself was now at the back of the attic at Aunty Vernice's house, which was a shame really but then Aunty Vernice must have had her reasons.

Some say it was the Obeah man who had killed Mum's mum by putting a spell on her that made her too proud for her own damn good. So when the doctor wrote out a death certificate saying she had died from heart failure brought on by the fact that her heart had a weak valve because she was born that way, no one believed him even though Dr Jones had been to the United States to do his training. The opening of the door and the screaming that followed immediately seemed to blur into one. James looked at the clock. Half-past one.

'Oh no, she's early,' thought James above the shrieking, as now the baby had woken and was adding its bit to the hullabaloo.

'Mama was hanging out some clothes at the time and your Aunty Vernice was chopping wood with the big axe. Apart from Papa, she was the only one who could lift the damn thing. The next thing I remember was Mrs Audain running into the yard shouting *Leesha dead Leesha dead*. I don't remember much after that,' Mum said that time in the sewing room just before joining in with Tina Turner singing 'River Deep Mountain High' without Ike.

The screaming was becoming too much so James decided it was a good time to leave. Besides, there might be something he could do if he was right about what was about to happen. If he remembered correctly, Mama's house was at the end of the lane and if he ran fast enough he could get there before Mama had asked her second eldest and not so pretty daughter called Vernice to chop some wood for the oven for tonight's cooking. James knew it would be okay to run out of the room in front of the screaming Mrs Orson because whenever he'd heard stories about Mum's mum dying no one ever said anything about a little boy running out of the room where they found the body.

James's nightmares were usually in slow motion, whether it was being tied to a railway track with no underpants on, or falling from the Empire State Building and the further you fell the further away the ground got and you'd fall for so long you'd end up underneath the bed. **James was having that same feeling of helplessness as he ran through the trees and bushes in what he thought was the right way to Mama's house. The bushes and trees became thicker and thicker and everything became darker and darker and James was just about to give up and burst into tears when suddenly everywhere cleared up and became a grass field. There about a hundred yards away was a house that looked exactly like Mama's house in the picture from the photo album. It was a lot like a barn with wooden planks for walls and large square holes where the windows should be. If it had been on** *The High Chaparral* **it would've been where they kept the horses. It didn't look big enough to feed chickens never mind raise a family of twenty children but it must have been or else he wouldn't have had so many aunties, uncles and cousins. He wouldn't have had a mum neither. If he ran fast enough he might reach there before they'd heard the news. So he set off like he was in a 100-metre final of the Olympic Games. Good job it wasn't the final because a minute later he was still running and the shack was getting no nearer.**

Another nightmare of James's was the night before the first day back to school after the summer holidays. No matter how much you tossed and turned and counted sheep you couldn't fall asleep and every little noise was a scary monster outside the door. And the last time you looked at the clock it said five to eleven and next it said ten past ten. **So no matter how fast James ran the shack seemed to be going further and further away. And now the grass was getting longer and longer until it was no longer grass but nettles, dandelions and thistles and eventually everything became so thick it was no different from the trees and bushes he'd escaped from just a minute ago.**

James sat down and examined the red bleeding patches that were once his knee caps. He'd had enough of all this running and getting nowhere. Besides, he didn't see why he had to hurry to save Aunty Vernice's finger. It was an accident, Mum said. Aunty Vernice had been chopping wood when Mrs Audain came running into the yard shouting *Leesha dead Leesha dead.* **It couldn't be helped really, it was a big axe, Mum said, and once you swung and it came down, that was it.**

It had been a while since Aunty Vernice had stopped visiting. Ever since Mum told her they were moving to Ashton-under-Lyne to live happily ever after. Aunty Vernice hadn't liked it one bit and she told everyone at the party just to make sure. 'She goes round like her shit don't stink,' she said in a loud voice so everyone upstairs could hear too. 'Just like her mother. Pretty and proud, yes, and look what happened to her.'

Mum did as she always did when shouted at. She pretended not to hear and got on with what she was doing at the time, which in this case was helping James with the food.

'Umm, cheese crackers, lovely.'

James couldn't see what all the fuss was about. It wasn't

as if they were going far. Three buses, Mum said, three buses. And there'd still be change from two bob. And if what Mum and Dad had said was true then it wasn't half as bad as **arriving here from the West Indies. On the sea in a big boat for three whole weeks, the first two weeks being sick as a dog. Then you'd have to get a train from the white cliffs of Dover all the way to Central Station in the pouring rain. It didn't stop there, oh no. If you were lucky then your uncle would meet you to take you on a trolley bus to his house and you'd have a really cold room on the top of a million stairs but it was okay because everyone else in the house was from the same village back home,** Dad said.

Or if you were unlucky there would be no one to meet you when you arrived at Central Station. So you would have to ask the nice policeman for directions to Number 10 Fairlawn Road, Moss Side, Manchester, which just so happened to be the address that was painted on your suitcase in case you got lost, Mum said. No definitely not. Moving to Ashton-under-Lyne was much easier, much easier by a long chalk, as Aunty Mary would say. So he couldn't see why Aunty Vernice was getting all hot and bothered for. Mum said they could visit any time they liked. But then grown-ups were like that, getting angry and jealous for absolutely no reason whatsoever. It was like at school and the rest of the class couldn't spell a word and they couldn't ask Miss Young because she was at a staff meeting or off sick yet again so instead there was a pretend teacher from somewhere else who didn't have a clue about anything. And the next time there was a spelling test with that word in extra specially and the only person who could spell it was James because of the encyclopedias Mum bought from the salesman who knocked on the door. Then everyone else would get really angry with James even though it wasn't his fault in the first place. Actually, thought James, this was nothing like Mum and Aunt Vernice and them not liking each other no more, but then just thinking that he would never have to go to Greenheys School no more once they moved to Ashton-under-Lyne made him feel glad all over.

James suddenly remembered the bottle the band-leader had given him. He felt his back pocket. Phew! Thank goodness it hadn't broken. He shook it once, chocolate. He shook it again, lemon cordial. Suddenly, the thick grass and bushes cleared away and there he was, in the backyard of the shack, sitting on the fence with his legs dangling down, exposing his red rare knee caps to the sun so by the time it was all over the blood would have turned to scabs and in no time at all the knees would be as brand new and he would be able to play football again. James could see everything from where he sat. The woman washing clothes in an old bath-tub, the little girl helping her, a young woman chopping wood on a tree stump and the gate at the end of the yard. James couldn't have had a better view if he'd been sat on the brand new sofa still wrapped in plastic all ready for the brand new house in Ashton-under-Lyne. So all he had to do was wait for Mrs Audain to come running into the yard.

thirty-one

'It's a pleasant change to watch someone else's funeral, I can tell you.'

It had been late at night with everyone in bed when the door bell rang. Then came the knocking and muffled shouts. James could hear Dad swearing as he put on his slippers and Mum telling him to be careful. Once there was no screaming as Dad opened the front door, James relaxed and would have fallen asleep if Dad hadn't called up to Mum to come down here quick it was Clarence.

James must have fallen asleep, as the next minute Mum was stood over him all dressed and in her outdoor coat with a face on like she'd seen a ghost. Felicia was sat on the bed still in her night-gown with a face like she knew what was up already. Now it was James's turn.

Mum sat down.

'Your Aunty Margaret's dead. Me and your father are going over to see what we can do. I've written a note so you don't have to go to school.'

And with that she got up and told Felicia what to do

while they were at Aunt Vernice's where the whole family had gathered by now to do whatever grown-ups did when one of them died of a heart attack at the really old age of thirty-nine years old.

It was the first real funeral James had been to. He'd been to Joey's, of course, but that was another story. There was everything in this one. Wailing relatives dressed in black, beating their chests whilst looking into the coffin to see if Aunty Margaret was still alive and walking away shaking their heads like they didn't believe it. Uncle Donald, her husband, stood standing in the corner with his hands in his pockets, even though it was his house. James didn't mind having to wear his Sunday-best suit. He wouldn't have missed this for the world.

Aunty Margaret had been Aunty Vernice's younger sister and, therefore, Mum's aunty, but you wouldn't have believed it by the way Mum talked about her. And whenever James did anything wrong or wouldn't do as he was told, she would say, 'You're worthless like your Aunty Margaret,' which meant you were good for nothing. Any time he didn't make his bed or wash the dishes or Hoover the stairs when he was supposed to. And if Mum was really vexed she would tell the story of the six foolish maids who forgot to put oil in their lamps while the six wise maids didn't forget. So when they were returning home at night from choir practice the six wise maids were able to get home safely whilst the six foolish maids got lost and were eaten by wolves. All because they didn't have oil in the lamps. And if Mum was really really vexed she would remind James that she had to be a wise maid because when you haven't a mother you were grateful for your grandmother to look after you and when you were told to clean the yard or wash the clothes or miss school and go to town to sell rum then you had absolutely no choice but to be a wise maid. And if Mum was really really really vexed she would also say that her Aunty Margaret could afford to be a foolish maid because Aunty Vernice would send her five-pound postal orders from England so she could go around having babies with Tom, Dick and Harry.

Things really got going at the church. It started off normally enough. Cushions on the benches so no one got a sore bum. A pile of hymn books so no one had an excuse for not singing. The vicar saying nice words about the woman in the coffin that sounded nothing like Aunty Margaret. Maybe he'd got the names mixed up with someone else. Then the trouble started. A wailing screech from the front bench and a bunch of people rushed forward like someone had thrown a ball into the middle. And there in the middle was Charlene, Margaret's eldest daughter, being held down before she did some more mischief. But that didn't stop her from thrashing about and screaming *Mama Mama*. By now everyone had stopped singing and were stretching their necks trying to get a better view, but the people on the front bench had Charlene under control. After clearing his throat the vicar continued with the nice words as if nothing had happened.

It was a big mistake having 'Rock of Ages' as a hymn at a funeral, because as soon as the singing began, Charlene broke free and ran up the steps to where the coffin was and threw herself at it like she was Gordon Banks. She would have knocked it over and spilt Aunty Margaret all over the floor if the vicar hadn't dashed round the back of the coffin and grabbed it with both arms. They took no chances after that. Charlene was taken out still sobbing *Mama* while everyone else had got to the third verse. Throughout all this Mum didn't sing or rush forward to help. All she said was, 'Damn you, Margaret,' but not loud enough for anyone to hear because even Mum knew this wasn't the right time to open up old wounds. There would be blood all over the place, knowing Mum. Besides, no one could possibly understand how angry she was with her Aunty Margaret, the foolish maid, for going off and dying like that and leaving everything in a right mess. Her husband, her children, the unpaid bills, brand new furniture still wrapped in polythene bags, more children back *home* with Tom, Dick and Harry.

'Damn you, Margaret. Damn you.'

But the best was still to come. After the service, everyone went to the cemetery to bury the body. Charlene decided she wanted to be buried too, so she threw herself into the hole with the coffin in, and she would have stayed there too if Dad and some other men hadn't jumped in after her and pulled her out. They took her to one of the black cars for some smelling salts. While all this was going on, Aunty Vernice led a chorus of 'Abide With Me'. She would say the words then the others would sing it, then she'd say the next line and they'd sing it and so on and so on. This went on for a long time because 'Abide With Me' was Aunty Vernice's favourite hymn. Those who weren't singing just stood around, some chatting and catching up on old times and others huddled in a group holding each other like they were about to fall over. Dad and some other men helped the diggers to fill the grave. Others just grabbed a handful of dirt and threw it in the grave. James looked up at Mum.

'Can I?' asked James and Mum nodded.

'Take Laura with you.' So James took Laura's hand and walked up to the edge of the hole. 'Be careful,' he could hear from behind. So he grabbed a handful of the muddiest dirt he could find, then rolled it into two balls and gave Laura one.

'We'll do it together, after three: one, two, three.'

James's bit hit the side first before landing near the bottom near to where her feet would have been if the top wasn't on. Laura's landed right on top of the name plate. It even went splat. They looked at each other and smiled. 'Nice shot.'

After that, everyone went back to Aunty Margaret's house for something to eat. But when they arrived no one could get through the front door because Clarence and Uncle Luke had blocked the entrance with furniture as if they were also moving to a brand new house in Ashton-under-Lyne which they weren't of course. They were taking them to a van outside which had its engine running. And in the living room, Aunty Vernice was arguing with some other grown-ups about the furniture even though it wasn't her house. And she stood in front of the brand new china cabinet that Aunty Margaret had bought only the week before from Piccadilly as it would be an ideal wedding present for Harriet and her fiancé even though she didn't know why her favourite daughter had to marry an African who was blacker than coal.

'If you think you can have any you've got another thing coming, Coolie,' said Aunty Vernice with an armful of cushions as she passed Mum in the entrance.

'Don't worry,' said Mum, 'I've no intention.'

The food table was in the room with the old furniture in that no one wanted. Sandwiches, sausages and pineapples on sticks, chicken – the usual stuff. But no one was eating, not even James. So it stayed there, as fresh as this morning when Deniece, Harriet and Colleen had made it up, just after choosing what things they wanted from Aunty Margaret's house. And all the adults just sat there like they couldn't wait to go home and have a bath. Some tried to talk, saying things like hasn't your daughter grown and how Margaret could eat mangoes without getting her hands sticky. But mostly they just stared at the mud on their shoes. And eventually Mum decided that this was a good time to go to Mr Hagen's office which was only down the road and collect the keys for their brand new house in Ashton-under-Lyne because the deposit was paid and everything so why don't the whole family go down to see Mr Hagen – it might be fun. But not before she picked up the little porcelain doll from the mantelpiece that she'd had her eyes on ever since Aunty Margaret bought it from Kendal's because Kendal's was where the rich white people went to do their shopping. Dad looked at Mum and shook his head and all Mum would say was, 'And why not, everyone else is.'

thirty-two

'The last one? Say something special? Okay James, try this for size: Scobie Breasley!'

All this thinking was giving James a headache real bad. There was so much to do. But it was so hard to get up after a nice dream and a dry bed. Before you knew it, it was eleven o'clock. Going to bed late the night before hadn't helped, with all the police sirens, windows breaking, people shouting, and everything. A group of young men had broken Mrs Best's front window for no reason whatsoever, and when she came out to tell them off, one of them had his hands over his head to stop the bleeding. That was when the police and ambulance arrived.

They'd been watching *The Avengers* at the time whilst eating a plate of salami and lettuce sandwiches and a big pot of tea. Only Felicia heard the glass breaking. By the time they'd run outside the lights in every front window were on and everyone was out on the street like a sunny summer's day. And even though Emma Peel had been in a bikini, James didn't mind in the slightest because everything outside was much better than the telly. The young men were pushing each other as the policemen talked into their walkie-talkies and the man with the bleeding head was sat down on the pavement with a head full of hankies. Dad would've told James and Laura to get back inside this minute but he was too busy with Mum and the other grown-ups to notice them sat on the pavement playing Scissors Bat Brick. And by the time Laura had won forty-five to thirty, the street was full of even more shiny faces and more flashing lights because an ambulance had arrived to take away the man with the bleeding head.

But now it was the morning after and if James had his way there wouldn't be enough time to play Scissors Bat Brick or anything like that. This was the last Sunday, the very last Sunday in Cadogen Street, Moss Side, Manchester. So whatever it was it had to be special, very special. But first things first. Breakfast!

Sirens again, just like last night. Only this time there'd been a loud bang before over in the direction of Alexandra Park. That was a very sensible idea. If a plane was going to crash in Moss Side then ideally it would be Alexandra Park as there was lots of grass and fields, even more than Platt Fields and the Rec. Mind you, the pilot would have to look out for the big lake. But from the sound of the bang and the big cloud of dust rising into the air it was obvious the pilot had got it right. James was about to run off in the direction of the cloud dust when the front door of Number 22 opened and Aunty Mary stepped out wearing a night-gown and slippers and holding two empty milk bottles.

'Do us a favour, pop over to the corner shop for a pack of Doctor Whites.'

Doctor Whites were packets of cotton wool strips. Women and big girls put them between their legs and when it turned red they would flush them down the toilets. James and his friends called them Jam Rags.

Aunty Mary took out her purse. 'Half a crown should be enough.'

'Aww, Aunty Mary.'

'It won't take a minute. Oh, and don't forget, large size please. Last time you got small size I had to stick two together with Sellotape.'

'Why can't you go yourself, it's not fair.'

'Couldn't cross me legs for weeks in case I got stuck.'

'Why can't you go?'

'Don't be silly, James, you know why. And anyway, haven't I helped you out enough lately.'

'I know you did but . . .'

'You can keep the change.'

'It was an accident.'

'I know, James.'

'I didn't mean to kill Joey.'

'I know, all you did was open the cage and Joey flew out.'

'You knew?'

'Of course I knew. Joey told me.'

'Joey told you?'

'Of course he did. I said he could talk, didn't I? Now off you go and don't forget, large size. I'm all out of tape and it's a right mess trying to peel it off from cotton wool, amongst other things.'

* * *

Mrs Powell looked at James as if he was mad.

'Are you sure you'll be okay?' And James said he would be even though the two ice-cream cornets were melting down his hands. He'd bought them when the man in the corner shop said he had no Doctor Whites left. And when he knocked on the door to give one to Aunty Mary, Mrs Powell answered the door instead which was just as well as it was her house in the first place.

'Yes, Mrs Powell. I thought you might like a cornet, that's all.'

'It's all right dear, but thanks all the same.'

And when she closed the door James could hear laughing and the sucking of teeth as grown-ups from back home do when they were having fun. There was no choice, he had to eat them both. Actually, it was never any choice but there was no harm in pretending. James was good at pretending. Even Mrs Rowbottom had said so. 'If pretending was an Olympic sport, young man, you'd have a dozen gold medals by now.' But it wasn't an Olympic sport so James had to make do like he always did. Maybe it would be easier in Ashton-under-Lyne, in a brand new semi-detached house with two trees, a front and back lawn and a garage even though they did not have a car.

Suddenly a Ford Anglia pulled up beside him and the man on the passenger seat wound down the window. 'I'll have one of those if you show us where the plane crashed.'

Days like this were like a favourite tune in your head, a favourite pop song or a tune you'd heard once before and you would only ever hear it again at extra special moments. Even before he'd seen the burnt out shell of the plane where it had crashed just yards from the edge of the lake in Alexandra Park, James knew that today was one of those days. Normally he would never get into cars with strangers. Not after what Mum, Dad and all the teachers had told him about the little girl and another boy who wasn't so little, neither of whom were ever seen again until they were found buried up the Moors. Normally James wouldn't get into cars with strangers but today wasn't normal. Besides, the man had a tape-recorder and a Scottish accent and the woman in the driver's seat was very pretty, with her blonde hair and black mascaraed eyes – she could've been on the telly if she wanted. All three of them were licking their fingers after sharing both of the ice-creams between them. James looked out the window. The streets were packed with people running in one direction, Alexandra Park, where the plane crashed. Then he saw Carl running along the other side of the road. The car stopped at the traffic lights. Carl ran up to the car.

'Oi you, I thought you'd left.'

'No, not yet.' said James.

Carl peered into the car and looked at the man fiddling with the tape-recorder. 'Hello sonny, want a lift?' said the man, trying very hard to be friendly but you could tell he wasn't.

'Come on luv, we won't bite,' said the woman as she stretched over to open the side door, bending over just enough to show the top of her bra.

'No thanks,' said Carl, then he turned to James. 'Want a game of marbles? I'll play you me ball bearing. You only have to hit twice to win.'

'Yeah, go on then.' And before the couple had a chance to say goodnight, God bless, James had dashed out of the car and was running after Carl, who had suddenly changed his mind about playing marbles and ran away instead.

After about a minute James had given up the chase. And even though Carl had tricked him, he was pleased he was out of the car. They looked a nice enough couple but there was something strange about them. The car smelt too, like someone had been digging up the garden. James had guessed they'd been digging because of the dirty spade on the back seat. So it was with some relief when Carl ran up to the car even though they still weren't speaking to each other ever since he had hit Carl in the face. He felt more a part of things being amongst the crowds, like he was part of something special. If he had stayed in the car he would've got there much sooner but then he would've missed all of the fun. The sun was as high in the sky as was possible and there wasn't a cloud in sight. And everyone looked so happy as they walked along. Smiling, chatting, holding hands, some with small kids on their shoulders. James recognised some of the faces. Mr and Mrs Turner with their daughter, Trudy, strolling along like they were the only family with one child and they wanted everyone to know. Errol was there with his sisters who were playfully punching him in the back as he ran in front of them and he had a smile on his face like he enjoyed being the youngest one in the family. And over the road were Mr and Mrs Cole with their seven daughters starting from the youngest, Maureen, who was in James's class, and ending with the oldest who James didn't know the name of. It was the first time James had seen Mr Cole, a small man with a bald patch and hair up his nostrils. Mrs Cole was big and fat as usual. James wished he'd stopped off and told Mum and Dad to come, even Felicia, Laura and Rose. But there was still a lot of packing to do and Mum had sent him out so as he wouldn't get under her feet. Felicia was helping because she was at the big school in Piccadilly. James didn't know where Laura was because he'd run out before Mum had insisted he should play with her. And Rose was still a toddler so she didn't matter. Even so, it would've been nice if they were here so they could hold his hands or even punch him in the back if he ran in front of them.

He felt a tap on his shoulder. It was Aunty Mary and she was in her Carmen Miranda dress again. 'Plastic fruit this time, the last lot went off. It'll do for the carnival, don't you think?'

'What carnival? I thought it was a plane crash.'

'Don't you know anything, silly? Once there's a plane crash, there has to be a carnival. It's a must, a pre-requisite.' And with that she ran ahead as fast as high heels would allow her. 'Meet you there, okay? Have to rush. Might be some bodies left over from the crash. They'll need a hand with what to do next. I know I did. Boy, the first few hours. Felt like death warmed up, I can tell you.'

Apart from the houses being bigger and more cars on the road, Princess Road was no different to any other road in Moss Side. It wasn't safe to play out, though. You'd get run over by a bus or car on its way to Piccadilly or Manchester Airport. It was okay for Aunty Vernice and Uncle Luke to live there though because all their children were grown-ups. Especially Clarence. He was still working in a garage fixing cars and bikes, making cups of tea and collecting Terry the Tiger stickers for James and his friends. Harriet was still a nurse in the building across the road from Greenheys School and Deniece, Benjamin and Colleen were still at the big school for grown-ups. Aunty Vernice insisted everyone had a photograph. And even though Princess Road was like any other road, it was perfect for parades and processions. Boys' Brigade marches every Whit Sunday, row upon row of dark blue uniforms and caps marching so exactly you could set your watches to them. And on Bonfire Night there would be bonfires all along the side streets that joined on to Princess Road. And if you were really lucky and Bonfire Night was on a Friday or Saturday then there would be enough time to see all of them because you didn't have to go to school tomorrow.

And as James joined in with the happy throng as they went on their merry way, he remembered the most favourite parade ever. James was only six at the time and it was the Friday before Bonfire Night. *The Avengers* was on the telly when suddenly there was a bang bang on the door and muffled voices shouting hurry up hurry up. Mum went to the door with a frying pan in case it was burglars but she didn't need it because it was Clarence, Harriet, Deniece, Benjamin and Colleen. And instead of taking a seat and having a cup of tea they said hurry up there was going to be a parade on Princess Road any minute now and guess who was in it yes Batman and Robin. James didn't believe them of course because Batman was his most favourite hero off the telly and favourite heroes did not come to Moss Side, especially on the Friday before Bonfire Night. But they insisted it was true and once they had convinced Mum to let him and Felicia go – Laura couldn't go because she was only a baby and Rose couldn't go because she wasn't born yet – it didn't take them long to run down Broadfield Road, across Westwood Road, down Raby Street, until finally running on to Princess Road where a big crowd had gathered already.

Princess Road was no different to any other road in Moss Side, apart from the small brick walls at the front with a gate and a small path that led up to the front door. This was perfect for waiting for parades, either on Clarence's shoulder or sat on the wall with your legs dangling down. Aunty Vernice made a jug of lemonade and just as Harriet poured out a glass for James a buzz went round the waiting crowd.

'He's coming, he's coming, oh my goodness.'

It wasn't Batman but it was the next best thing. It was a big parade of brass bands and dancing ladies followed by a big open truck full of Batman's Supervillains. The Joker, the Riddler, the Penguin and even Catwoman. There were a few others as well but James didn't recognise them. And they smiled and waved so much you would never believe that one of them had tied both Batman and Robin head first and upside down over a tub of boiling oil with only a string next to a burning candle stopping them from falling in. James was so happy he could've gone home and gone straight to bed and fallen asleep right away. But he couldn't of course because Batman and Robin hadn't come yet and even though there were a load of other trucks with lights going past, none of them had Batman or Robin in. But it was okay by James because there was enough to see and smell in the Princess Road after seven o'clock in the evening. The row of houses on the other side of the road that were lit up with fluorescent light bulbs and net curtains. The neon lights of shops with names like Yates's

Wine Lodge and Barry's Men's Outfitter's. The shop with boarded up windows where some of Dad's friends would play dominoes and drink rum. The sweet shop owned by Mr Meskies when he wasn't the ice-cream man. The smell of banana fritters and saltfish cakes frying in someone's kitchen. And if you looked up into the sky, the smog stopped you from seeing the moon or any of the stars because in those days they didn't have smokeless coal ...

And now all these years later, as James walked along the same Princess Road, he knew he wanted this last Sunday to feel exactly like that time all those years ago even though when Batman and Robin eventually did arrive it was almost impossible to see them because the crowd pushed forward to block the view. And when he did manage to see them James knew they weren't the real Batman and Robin because the Batmobile had English number plates.

A crowd of people walking was a strange thing, James decided. You could be in the middle of a crowd so close that when you stuck out your arm you'd hit someone in the face. Even so you'd still feel as if you were the only person in the world. Not unhappy alone but alone all the same. So alone you could talk to yourself or pick your nose and no one would tell you to stop it. And when you didn't want to be alone any more all you had to do was put your hands up and there was someone to talk to, such as Vincent from Number 12 who was riding his brand new Raleigh bike.

'I thought you'd left?'

'Nah, not yet.'

'Wanna lift?'

'Nah, I wanna see all the fun. See you there.'

But Vincent hadn't heard the last bit because he'd peddled off as soon as James had said, 'Nah.'

And just in case he got bored Aunty Mary turned up again. She was still in her Carmen Miranda outfit but this time she was holding a pair of maracas. And as usual she had a lot to say for herself. But not before she had a shake on the maracas. 'I love a good shake, don't you? Helps clear the sinuses.'

She shook them again.

'I knew there was something missing but I couldn't quite remember. Good job I got back in time. These were the only pair left.'

Another shake.

'Now young man, I believe you have a question for me.'

James wanted to say how did you guess but then again that was Aunty Mary for you. He cleared his throat, it was a hard enough question as it was without him getting it all mixed up. 'Aunty Mary?'

'Yes dear.'

'Is it true what they say about Louise's mum Miriam? Did she really swallow a whole bottle of aspirin all by herself?'

'Yes dear, and a bottle of whisky.'

'A bottle of whisky, wow, I didn't know that.'

'Johnnie Walker, she was always partial to a drop of Johnnie's. A waste of good whisky if you ask me. Oh and that isn't the half of it neither, James.'

'So it's true then?'

'You know, don't you. Oh dear.'

'Our Felicia said she did it because she was pregnant with a coloured man's baby.'

'Bad news travels fast, eh?'

'Seems daft if you ask me, Aunty Mary. I mean, once you're dead that's it. There's no coming back.'

'You're right there, young man.'

'So it's daft really when you do it yourself. I think so, don't you?'

'It's only the living you have to be scared of, not the dead.'

'Aunty Mary? You all right?'

'Sorry James, I don't know what came over me for a moment there.'

Then she shook her maracas twice, shake shake.

James held his hand out. 'Can I have a go?'

Mary looked at her watch. 'Can't stop. The man said to return it by one o'clock or else I lose me deposit.' Then she patted James on the head. 'Think of this day as if it was a really long poo. You know the kind. Where your stomach aches from last night's fish and chips supper and you wait until the afternoon with your bum clenched tight, and then when the time is right you run to the toilet, undo your stockings, pull down your knickers and then Ahhh Bisto.'

James tried to imagine Aunty Mary walking around with her legs crossed and a squirm on her face but he'd only had breakfast two hours ago so he thought better not.

James approached the big iron gates of Alexandra Park. Someone had painted the gates in psychedelic colours and tied on ribbons and flowers just like Harvest Festival. And there along the path from the gates was a row of multicoloured stalls just like Denmark Road Market used to be before it closed down. Each stall had a hand-painted sign saying what was sold. Fried chicken with rice'n'peas, saltfish cakes, banana fritters, meat patties, rum and blackcurrant, Davenport's Brown Ale, fried fish with the bones left on. James stood and stared at the sign saying curried goat and rice. Mrs Best from next door was behind the stall, stirring a big metal pot over an oil heater. James had never tasted curried goat before, he didn't think it was allowed to eat goats never mind curried ones. He wondered if there were any horns in the pot. Mrs Best ladled some into a small bowl.

'Here, try some.'

Curried goat my foot, thought James. He knew mutton when he tasted it. But he was too polite to say anything. Besides, his mouth was on fire. What he needed was a cold drink and fast, right now even. And as James set off in search of a drink he had no time to notice the other stalls playing 'The Israelites' by Desmond Decker and 'I Heard it Through the Grapevine' by Marvin Gaye, both at the same time. Normally, he would stop, listen and go off into a world of his own. But now wasn't normal and what he needed right now was a glass, no, a bucket of ice-cold water, to quench the fire in the hole that was once his mouth.

So when Aunty Mary reappeared in a red and white apron behind a stall saying CRUSHED ICE especially for burnt mouths and sore bums, James wasn't the least bit surprised. She even held the cup to his mouth as he slurped the melted ice.

'I'm sorry, James. You must think me a stupid old fool at times. It's just that there's nothing to do up there and it's not every day you have the chance to play the maracas.' She shook them but no sound came out of them. She held them up to her face and smiled. 'I know exactly how you feel. Don't worry, won't be long now.' Then she turned to James. 'You know what I miss the most, it's a nice cheese and Marmite sandwich with pickled onions and peanut butter. White bread of course, with the crust cut off. Blue Band margarine as well, it has to be Blue Band. I never told you, did I, that I preferred Blue Band to butter. Keep it under your hat, I've my reputation to think about.'

And if James had known this would be the last time he would ever see her again then he would've said something special or even said goodbye. But he didn't know so he just stood there with his mouth open, like he was trying to catch flies.

James felt a slap across his head and when he turned round, there was Errol. 'Come on, stupid, hurry or you'll miss everything.' And when he turned back to tell Aunty Mary that he missed her too, she'd gone. All that remained was the stall and buckets of ice. If James had known then that he would never see her ever again he would've said something special, maybe even kissed her on the cheek. But he didn't know, so he ran after Errol instead, who had disappeared amongst the crowd.

The image of the bright red sun was the last thing on James's mind as he fluffed up his pillow and closed his eyes. A bright red sun the size of a big balloon like it did when something special was about to happen. Only one steel band played at first. Then another joined in, then another, then another, until eventually the air was filled with the sounds of so many bands it sounded like one great big one. It was so good that everyone stopped what they were doing, listened for a while, before some of them

decided to dance again even though it wasn't Saturday night. The bright red sun, the steel bands and burnt out shell of the BEA aeroplane just like the one that crashed in Munich with all the Manchester United players still on board. Then again, it could have been the one that crashed in Stockport a few years ago on the *Six O'Clock News,* **or even the plane crash on** *Emergency Ward Ten* **on the telly last week. They all looked the same as far as James was concerned.**

It all ended perfectly when Mum and Dad came to collect James who was sat down on the ground pulling daisies from the grass and humming the tune one of the steel bands had played.

' "St Kitts at Night",' said Dad to Mum as they slowly crept up to James. 'They used to play that tune every carnival.' Then he gently patted James to come on home everyone's been worried sick.

Mum just smiled as she wiped a grass stain from James's cheek.

'It's not time for bed yet,' said James, his bum wet from the damp grass.

Mum and Dad smiled. 'Come on, young man. The sooner we get you home the sooner we can get on with the packing.'

'Can I help?'

'No, young man. It's dinner for you then it's straight to bed. Up the stairs, apples and pears.'

'It's all right,' said James. 'I've eaten already.'

And he had too. Another bowl of curried goat and rice, two banana fritters, three saltfish cakes and a can of cola and a sherbet dip. He would've ate more but he was far too busy serving cups of lemon fudgesicles to anyone

who wanted. Which was practically anyone from back home who happened to be in Alexandra Park at the time. Which was practically the whole of Moss Side. It was just after Aunty Mary had left for the last time. He couldn't find Errol so he went back to the stall where she had served him a cup of ice.

The steel bands were still playing when Mrs Powell danced up to the stall with a bottle of orange pop in one hand and a chicken leg in the other. 'Just like carnival,' she said and she kissed James on the forehead, leaving a big red lipstick mark right in the middle. 'Give me some of your ice for me drink, dear.'

As she poured the orange pop into a cup of ice, the steel band music slowly changed to the sound of beating drums. Drum drum drum, like a heartbeat. Drum drum drum, like Mum's sewing machine too. Drum drum drum. And everyone danced, even Mrs Powell, like they'd been doing it all their lives. Drum drum drum. Not like the Africans on the telly, more like a soft shoe shuffle down the road. Some were so good they could turn around and do a full circle, talk about the weather, what was on the telly tonight, had anyone died, and eat a bowl of soup, all at the same time.

'That's better,' said Mrs Powell, gulping down the last chunk of ice from the cup. 'Almost as good as lemon popsicles, but not quite.'

And when Dad asked James if he'd had a good day, James told him he'd had some lemon fudgesicles and both Mum and Dad laughed and Mum patted James on the head just as they turned round the corner from Broadfield Road on to Cadogen Street.

'If we hurry, we'll see the end of *Bonanza*.'

'*Bonanza* isn't on Sundays.'

'It is now, said so in the paper,' said Dad.

After Mrs Powell had shuffled away, a big long queue had formed in front of James's stall, and all of them were shuffling on the spot as the drum drum drumming was still going on. If James had his way he would've stayed there forever and ever amen, just watching them shuffle on the spot. Much better than Pan's People on *Top of the Pops*. But the ones at the front of the queue would have none of it. They were there for only one thing.

'A fudgesicle please.'

And James was about to say I haven't got none so go away and leave me alone please, when Mrs Carnes pointed to the bottle sticking out of James's pocket. 'What's that sticking out of your pocket?'

Some asked for a lemon popsicle which meant one shake of the bottle, and others wanted a fudgesicle please – two shakes – but no one asked for a lemon fudgesicle because that was just ridiculous. Everyone said they remembered lemon popsicles and fudgesicles being on a stick just like an ice lolly but it tasted just as nice from a cup, thank you very much. And whilst they sipped on their cups, they either danced to the drum drumming of the drums, had something else to eat from one of the other stalls, or went over and had a look at the burnt out wreck of the plane.

Once upon a time on the island of St Kitts there was a young coloured woman called Felicia who was very pretty and very proud indeed because she had long black shiny hair. And although she could have any man she wanted, she chose a fisherman called John to have a baby with. She called the baby Veronica even though she didn't marry the fisherman called John, who was also a carpenter when fishing was poor. And because she was so very proud she couldn't go back to her family of a mother and father, two sisters, Vernice and Margaret, and a brother called Nathan. Instead she made a vow to marry the next man that came along. And at the time she thought she was very very lucky indeed when the next man to come along was a mulatto who had a job in the bank. And the mulatto man who had a job in the bank was even more pleased to marry Felicia but only on the condition that Veronica went to live with her grandmother, which as far as Felicia was concerned was okay by her because if truth be known she'd had little time for her little daughter called Veronica. Eventually she had a child by the mulatto man who had a job in the bank, a little boy called Samuel. But that didn't stop him from sending Felicia to work as a maid for Mr Orson, the estate owner. That was where they found her dead on Mr Orson's leather settee with a baby in her arms. Even now whenever the subject is brought up, those old enough to remember just turn their heads and pretend nothing ever happened in the first place.

Baby Samuel went to stay with his father from the bank who by now had found himself another woman to live with, but only on the one condition that it was okay to keep little Samuel but it was still not okay to keep another woman's daughter, no sirree. Which was fine as far as Veronica was concerned because by now she was calling her grandmother Mama like she was really her mother. And eventually even Vernice came round to the idea of having Veronica about the place, especially when things needed doing like rising every morning with the cock crows before school to sell bottles of rum to the workers in the cane field. And when Vernice married Luke from town and had Clarence Harriet Deniece Benjamin and Colleen, having Veronica around to do all the housework was an absolute godsend. And when she and Luke went off to England like everyone else, Vernice thought it would be okay to leave things as they were. So you could imagine everyone's disappointment when Veronica found out she was pregnant when she was only fifteen – oh no, not Veronica, anyone else maybe but not *Veronica*. But as far as Veronica was concerned, getting pregnant was a blessing in disguise. For a start, it meant she no longer had to go to school which was a relief really because she'd missed so much of it beforehand through selling rum, cutting cane and looking after Aunt Vernice's children, that the school teachers had thought she'd left already and gone to the States. However, no one was surprised neither when she called the baby Felicia, after her mother and grandmother.

It had started off as a joke really. Uncle Luke had thought it was a good idea to marry off Veronica to the nearest fellow who could afford it. Everyone laughed at the time, even Aunt Vernice. Even so, Patrick from down the road came visiting more often than once. His parents owned the bread shop down the road and he always wore shoes to school. But that soon ended once Uncle Luke and Aunt Vernice went over to England. Veronica made sure of that. And when Aunty Vernice sent the boat fare for Veronica to come to England to live with her and Uncle Luke in a big house on Princess Road in Moss Side, Manchester, it had been such a long time since Uncle Luke had told the joke that everyone had forgotten it by now. But Aunt Vernice had no intention of letting Veronica forget about her responsibilities back home. So every month like clockwork, Veronica would send a postal order to Mama in order to buy milk powder and nappies for her little baby Felicia.

Veronica loved being in England. There was so much to do in England. There was always work, and not even just in crop season, there was no such thing as crop season in England. And there were so many shops in England where you could buy anything you liked, you didn't have to be friends with such and such neither. In England you didn't have to wait for Mrs Michaels to kill one of her cows to buy some meat. All you did was to go into the shop and say I'll have that piece there Mr Miles and the butcher would cut it up and wrap it then he put it in your basket between the eggs and the cornflakes, it was that simple. You'd be asked for money afterwards but that was a small price to pay.

And at work she met a fellow, a nice young man from Nevis called Raymond, or Smallie to his friends. He was called Smallie because he never talked much. And when he did talk it was only to tell her that he played cricket every Sunday and also sent postal orders to his mother. He also told her about mending fences and whitewashing the walls for Mr Henderson because his own son wore shoes to school. Veronica knew she loved Raymond when she saw him crying in the canteen, all because the plane with the Manchester United football team had crashed into a snow-covered field in Munich. It wasn't as if he knew them or anything. He'd only ever seen them on the telly for goodness sake. But still, it showed he cared, Mum said. It was then she decided that he would make an excellent father for her child, whether he liked it or not.

Things were happy for a while for Veronica and it stayed that way until she told her aunt that she wanted to be a nurse. Aunty Vernice said it was out of the question because there wasn't enough pay being a nurse and did she forget she had a baby to send postal orders for every month? It was then that Aunt Vernice reminded Veronica of Uncle Luke's joke, you know, the one about marrying her off to the nearest fellow who could afford it. Only this time no one was laughing. And things got worse when Uncle Luke mistook Veronica's bedroom for his. The first time it happened he said it was a mistake. But when it happened again the next Wednesday, and the next, Veronica got so fed up she told her aunt what was happening. But her aunt didn't believe her and started to beat Veronica and said you're just like your mother and Aunt Vernice didn't stop even when Veronica told her aunt she was going to get married. So the very next day Veronica went to the police station where the nice policewoman gave her a nice cup of tea and sent her over to see a probation officer who then told Veronica she would need her mother's death certificate if she wanted to marry Raymond without her aunt's permission. So Veronica went back to her aunt's house because she knew her aunt kept photos of her mother in a suitcase on top of a wardrobe and maybe the certificate might be there as well. But Aunt Vernice caught her before she could open the lock with a screwdriver. And Aunt Vernice really went mad at Veronica for opening up all kinds of old wounds as well as the suitcase. As far as Veronica was concerned, that was the final straw. So she went straight over to Raymond's room that very minute where she found him cooking a big panful of baked beans and scrambled eggs. And she stayed there until a copy of the death certificate finally arrived from the town hall in St Kitts. Then they got married at Christ Church on Monton

Street and bought a small terrace house on Cadogen Street with mice in the kitchen and cockroaches in the bathroom because there wasn't enough space for the two of them in Raymond's room, never mind the brand new baby boy that was expected at the end of the summer.

Mrs Ryan always said that James would make a good storyteller. And he was quick too. He'd managed to tell the whole story to himself from the time they left the park gates to just as they crossed over from Broadfield Road to the top of Cadogen Street. If Aunty Mary was here he would've told her of course. But she wasn't so he had to talk in his head instead. Which was just as well because he was sure he got some bits wrong. He'd even made some of it up when he couldn't remember what Mum had said. It wasn't his fault. She never ever told him the whole story in one go, just bits and pieces here and there, when she was in the sewing room and there was nothing good on the radio. And sometimes she would stop sewing and just stare at the wall for a few seconds.

And when Dad opened the front door with his key, Felicia had to climb over all the boxes and wrapped up furniture that blocked the entrance before she could rush up to meet them to say *Thank God* and Laura ran down the carpet-less stairs in her vest and knickers because her pyjamas had been packed away in one of the many suitcases in the front room. And while all this was going on, Rose lay fast asleep in her brand new cot bought especially for the brand new semi-detached house with a front lawn and a tree, a garage with a shared drive, two bedrooms and a box-room, venetian blinds, a kitchen hatch to pass the dinners through and shiny white tiles in the bathroom.

If Aunty Mary had been there she would have been really

pleased because everything was turning out just fine and dandy. Even so, there was loads more packing to do. The delivery van was due tomorrow morning at eight o'clock sharp and everything had to be ready or else. And if everything went to plan, by tomorrow evening the only thing left would be for everyone to sit down in front of the telly with their slippers off, a cup of tea and a plate of digestives and settle down for their first night in their brand new home in Ashton-under-Lyne, Lancashire, and live happily ever after . . .

For Ever and Ever, Amen.

*If you enjoyed this book here is a selection of
other bestselling titles from Review*

MY FIRST SONY	Benny Barbash	£6.99 ☐
THE CATASTROPHIST	Ronan Bennett	£6.99 ☐
WRACK	James Bradley	£6.99 ☐
IT COULD HAPPEN TO YOU	Isla Dewar	£6.99 ☐
ITCHYCOOBLUE	Des Dillon	£6.99 ☐
MAN OR MANGO	Lucy Ellmann	£6.99 ☐
THE JOURNAL OF MRS PEPYS	Sara George	£6.99 ☐
THE MANY LIVES & SECRET SORROWS OF JOSÉPHINE B.	Sandra Gulland	£6.99 ☐
TWO MOONS	Jennifer Johnston	£6.99 ☐
NOISE	Jonathan Myerson	£6.99 ☐
UNDERTOW	Emlyn Rees	£6.99 ☐
THE SILVER RIVER	Ben Richards	£6.99 ☐
BREAKUP	Catherine Texier	£6.99 ☐

Headline books are available at your local bookshop or newsagent. Alternatively, books can be ordered direct from the publisher. Just tick the titles you want and fill in the form below. Prices and availability subject to change without notice.

Buy four books from the selection above and get free postage and packaging and delivery within 48 hours. Just send a cheque or postal order made payable to Bookpoint Ltd to the value of the total cover price of the four books. Alternatively, if you wish to buy fewer than four books the following postage and packaging applies:

UK and BFPO £4.30 for one book; £6.30 for two books; £8.30 for three books.

Overseas and Eire: £4.80 for one book; £7.10 for 2 or 3 books (surface mail).

Please enclose a cheque or postal order made payable to *Bookpoint Limited*, and send to: Headline Publishing Ltd, 39 Milton Park, Abingdon, OXON OX14 4TD, UK.
Email Address: orders@bookpoint.co.uk

If you would prefer to pay by credit card, our call team would be delighted to take your order by telephone. Our direct line is 01235 400 414 (lines open 9.00 am–6.00 pm Monday to Saturday 24 hour message answering service). Alternatively you can send a fax on 01235 400 454.

Name ....

Address ....

....

....

If you would prefer to pay by credit card, please complete:
Please debit my Visa/Access/Diner's Card/American Express (delete as applicable) card number:

| | | | | | | | | | | | | | | | |

Signature .... Expiry Date..............